FORCING
THE ACE

orca limelights

FORCING THE ACE

Erin Thomas

ORCA BOOK PUBLISHERS

Library and Archives Canada Cataloguing in Publication

Thomas, E. L. (Erin L.), author
Forcing the ace / Erin Thomas.
(Orca limelights)

Issued in print and electronic formats.
ISBN 978-1-4598-0645-0 (pbk.).--ISBN 978-1-4598-0646-7 (pdf).--
ISBN 978-1-4598-0629-0 (epub)

I. Title. II. Series: Orca limelights
PS8639.H572F67 2014   jc813'.6   c2014-901557-7
c2014-901558-5

First published in the United States, 2014
Library of Congress Control Number: 2014935378

Summary: Alex wants to enter a magic competition, but first he'll have to
learn to share the spotlight with a rival magician.

MIX
Paper from
responsible sources
FSC® C103214

*Orca Book Publishers is dedicated to preserving the environment and has
printed this book on Forest Stewardship Council® certified paper.*

Orca Book Publishers gratefully acknowledges the support for
its publishing programs provided by the following agencies:
the Government of Canada through the Canada Book Fund and the
Canada Council for the Arts, and the Province of British Columbia
through the BC Arts Council and the Book Publishing Tax Credit.

Cover design by Rachel Page
Cover photography by Getty Images

ORCA BOOK PUBLISHERS
PO Box 5626, STN. B
Victoria, BC Canada
V8R 6S4

ORCA BOOK PUBLISHERS
PO Box 468
Custer, WA USA
98240-0468

www.orcabook.com
Printed and bound in Canada.

17 16 15 14 • 4 3 2 1

To the kids at magic camp,
and in loving memory of Y.C.

One

My hands are shaking. It's good that I'm not planning to saw anyone in half.

I'm backstage, behind those crusty green velvet curtains in the school auditorium, listening to the audience cheer for the hip-hop dance routine that just finished. There's a cardboard heart on the floor, shiny red marked with dusty shoe treads, left over from Valentine's Day last week. I take a deep breath and wipe my hands on my lab coat.

It's not like it's my first show. I know what I'm doing—mostly. It's my Weird Science routine. The finale is new, but that's good, because it means Donna hasn't seen it before.

Mrs. Forsythe, my English teacher, is onstage, her Jamaican accent as warm as buttered toast.

"And now, to prove once and for all that Thornton's Got Talent, Alex Eisen!"

Usually when she says my full name like that, it means another failed English quiz: *Alex Eisen, please see me after class.*

"That's you! Go!" It's one of the hip-hop dancers.

I grab the silver briefcase with my props inside and take another deep breath. The dancer shoves me, and I stumble onto the stage.

Spotlights warm my face. I blink into the light and set my case down on the little side table the stage crew set out for me. Straighten. Smile into the applause.

"Good evening, class," I say as the applause fades. "Welcome to remedial science one-oh-one. That is, er...science for dummies."

There's laughter. Good.

I open the briefcase and pull out the text-book that's sitting on top. When I open the book, a playing card pops up between the pages, like a bookmark. And when I pull it out, it appears to turn into a whole fan of cards. I stare at it, faking surprise, then shake my hand and drop the cards to the stage floor, but another fan of cards appears in my hand.

"The important thing to remember about science," I say, shaking free of the second fan, "is that there's a logical explanation for everything."

More laughter. From the stage, I can see the first few audience rows past the spotlights. My friend Hakim sits in one of the four front-row seats I bought. Donna's there too, wearing what might pass as a respectable suit if it weren't made of hot-pink vinyl. I throw in an extra card flourish just for her. She's the one I need to impress if I want her to sponsor me for the Silver Stage magic competition.

The other two seats, the ones for my parents, are empty. They didn't promise to be here, only to stop by if they could get out of their charity dinner early.

It shouldn't bother me.

Hakim waves, and I realize that I'm staring at the empty seats and my hands have gone still.

I clear my throat. "Let's talk about Newton," I say. "He discovered the law of gravity. Things fall down instead of up." I dribble the cards from my upper hand to my lower hand. "But what if Newton was wrong?" I spring the cards from my lower hand to my upper hand in a kind of reverse waterfall. "Newton wasn't into cards though—he was into apples." I pull one from my lab-coat pocket.

Apple on table. Red handkerchief over apple. Hidden under the handkerchief, the apple flies up off the table and around the stage. I pretend to chase it with my hands, trying to catch it, holding the back corners of the handkerchief. The audience's laughter sits in my belly, a warm ball. Finally I let the apple land. I tug away the handkerchief and bite into the apple. "Not bad," I say.

Applause. They're on my side now. They want to believe, so I give them things to believe in. A card torn to pieces, then restored: conservation of matter. A coin that passes through a bottle: proof that atoms are mostly space. Some of these tricks aren't great for such a large room, but Donna's right in the front row.

Sooner than feels possible, it's time for the finale. I swallow past a sudden tightness in my throat. This trick I haven't tried in front of an audience before. I wanted something flashy, something to show Donna that I'm not afraid to take risks.

"For this final trick," I say, "I'll need a volunteer."

Hakim waves his hands around like we planned. I scan the room, pretending to look for just the right person. And that's when I see her.

Zoe O'Neill is in the third row, and her hand is sliding up. Her smile just about takes me out at the knees.

"Zoe?" I'm not sure I've said her name out loud before. She's new this semester. I know, because the day she showed up in my chemistry class, I went home and scanned the old yearbooks to see why I'd never noticed her.

She starts to stand. Hakim's half out of his chair already, so I catch his eye and shake my head. He blinks a few times, then drops back to his seat.

I rub my thumb over the Band-Aid around the base of my middle finger, checking that the magnet is still hidden there—my backup plan. It'll be better this way, since Donna would know Hakim was a plant.

Zoe walks toward me. The spotlight finds her and turns her hair silver. To give her time to climb the steps to the stage, I pull out my cards again and play with them, except my hand stiffens and the cards fall. My face heats up.

I kneel to collect the cards. "I wanted to do that one last time, just in case. Extreme card manipulation. No tricks, just steady hands. And my hand"—I hold out my right hand, palm out, fingers spread—"is what's at stake now."

Zoe reaches the stage. She crouches across from me and picks up a couple of cards from the mess on the stage floor. She starts to pass them to me, but as I reach for them, she back-palms them. From the audience's angle, it must look like they just disappeared.

Zoe's a magician?

I take Zoe's hand between mine and slip the cards into my lab-coat pocket. There's applause as we stand, and I bow as if the disappearing cards were my doing. Inside, I'm reeling.

From my briefcase, I pull out four lumps of Plasticine and set them on the table, all in a row. Behind each one goes a tall Styrofoam cup. I hold up a stainless steel paring knife—a small one—and turn it so the spotlight glints off the blade.

"For every action, there is an equal and opposite reaction. I push down, the knife pushes up. Zoe will place the knife in one of these lumps of Plasticine, pointy end up. Then she'll cover all four lumps of Plasticine with the Styrofoam cups. I'm going to read her mind to figure out which one it is and then crush three cups with my hand. Hopefully, the right three."

Hakim was supposed to score the top of the knife cup with his fingernail. In case that didn't work, I had the magnet. It worked at home when I tested it—I could feel the tug of the knife, faintly, through the Styrofoam. But my hands are nervous now, my pulse heavy in my wrist.

I slice the apple with the knife to show that it's sharp, then hand the knife to Zoe. Her hands are steady as she takes it. Mine aren't.

I turn my back to the audience while she plants the knife.

"You can turn around now," she says.

The cups are lined up in a row. There's a small nick out of the top of the third cup, but I can't tell if Zoe did it on purpose.

"Use her hand," some jerk yells. Someone else picks up the shout.

My mouth is dry. I swallow. "That isn't—"

"It's all right," Zoe whispers. She reaches out her hand.

I'm sweating. "You don't want that," I tell the now-restless audience. "She could signal me where the knife is." I tug at my collar. This is the part where I'm supposed to look into Zoe's eyes and pretend to lift the memory from her mind.

Someone boos.

I take Zoe's hands. "Look at me." Her eyes are blue and very bright. "I think I see...yes. There it is."

She squeezes my hand three times.

I let go. Obligingly, Zoe stumbles a bit, blinking as if she's been through something. There's a hush from the audience.

I move to the table and hold my hand flat over the first cup—the one on my right, the audience's left. There's no tug on the magnet. "One." I smash my hand down, crushing the cup.

They're quiet now. Waiting. If I read Zoe's signal right, the knife is under the third cup. But third from which side?

I smash the cup on the far side. "Two." Two gone, the two in the middle left. A fifty-fifty chance. I let my hand hover over each one in turn, but if the magnet's sending a hint, I'm not getting it.

"Use my hand," Zoe says. Her voice is pinched.

Before she can move closer, before the audience can pick up on the idea again, I squeeze my eyes shut and crush my hand down on the cup on the left, the one with no mark on top.

The Styrofoam crumples. There's no pain at first. And then it rushes in, hot and sharp, spiking up my arm.

There's a gasp from the audience, and Zoe's shriek rising above it. "Alex!"

I open my eyes. The cup is crushed beneath my palm. A line of blood spreads from where the knife has sliced into my ring finger. Zoe's eyes are wide, her face pale as she stares at my hand.

I smile at the audience as if this were my plan all along. "Found it."

Two

"That was stupid, Alex. Really stupid," Dad says as we drive home from the emergency room. He's a surgeon at the children's hospital, so I think he's upset that someone else got to stitch me up.

I lean my head against the headrest in the backseat of his Prius. Streetlights flash by on the highway. He's going too fast, especially since it's snowing, but for once Mom isn't calling him on it.

It's late. So late that I'm feeling loose and reckless; we must have waited in the ER for two hours, and that was before Dad got into doctor mode and turned a quick trip for stitches into a full-on medical consultation.

The side of my ring finger is numb, and it doesn't bend easily: minor nerve damage they told me. Feeling and movement should come back on their own in a few weeks.

Weeks. The Silver Stage Magic Competition is still months away, but I can't afford to lose weeks of practice time. Thinking about it, I groan.

Mom looks over her shoulder at me, leaning around the seat. "Does it hurt?"

"He'll be fine," Dad says.

"I can answer for myself."

Dad grunts. The car accelerates.

"Brian," Mom warns.

I study my hands. They're long and narrow, like Dad's on the steering wheel. Surgeon's hands. Except that now two of the fingers on my right hand are taped together.

There wasn't even a chance to talk to Donna after the show. Mrs. Forsythe whisked me into the office, did her own magic with the first-aid kit and called my parents.

"At least this will be the end of it for a while," Dad says.

It takes a minute for his words to sink in. "Wait—what do you mean?"

"You can't be flipping cards with a bandaged hand. Maybe now you'll get some studying done. Don't you have a chemistry test coming up?"

"Brian," Mom warns.

He's right, but I scowl out the window instead of answering. "If I keep practicing, it won't stiffen up, right?" I ask. "I mean, if I keep moving my fingers, it's like physio, right?"

"Do I look like a physiotherapist to you?" he asks.

Which raises a question about what a physiotherapist looks like, but I know better than to say so.

Dad sighs. "You're in grade eleven, Alex. It's time to get serious. You think the colleges will take you because you can pull a rabbit out of a hat?"

"Did you see a rabbit in my act? Oh, wait. You weren't there."

"That's enough," Mom says. "It's late. Alex, you're hurt, but don't talk back to your father. And Brian, don't lash out at Alex just because you were scared."

Scared? Inconvenienced, more like. I slouch in my seat.

"What, I can't ask what he's planning to do with his life?"

"Physiotherapist," I flip back. Which makes him mad enough that the rest of the drive home is quiet.

The fact that I came in third in the talent show—which is kind of a big deal at my school—isn't even on anyone's radar.

* * *

At the magic shop, Donna wipes dust off a volume of *Tarbell Course in Magic*. It's fatter than my math and chemistry textbooks fused together.

"Good show last night, up until the end." Today she's wearing a velvet jumpsuit. It's a bit weird that someone as old as my mom still dresses like Catwoman, but that's Donna. With her spiky heels on, she's taller than me. "How's the hand? Are you going to be okay?"

I nod. "I'll need a new finale."

"The spike is not your friend," she deadpans. "It didn't really fit the act, either, but I think you knew that. You were trying to force a win instead of putting on a show. What gives?"

I shrug. "Just trying something new." Her Silver Stage certificate is beside me, up on the front wall near the books on card tricks. The frame's tarnished silver is shiny in the corner where we all rub it for luck.

The Silver Stage is *the* professional society for magicians. Donna earned her membership back in the nineties, when she had frighteningly large hair and a solo act in Vegas.

She's watching, but I close my eyes anyhow as I run my thumb over the corner of the frame and picture my future: Alex Eisen, World Champion Magician.

Donna is still a Silver Stage member in good standing, so she can sponsor me to enter the New Talent competition. It's here in Vancouver this year, which is awesome, because usually the competitions are too far away for me to get to.

"Donna, I—"

The phone rings. Donna waves a hand as she goes to answer it. "Have a look around. You'll think of something."

I sigh and flip through a book on card tricks: *The Expert at the Card Table*, by S.W. Erdnase. It's basically the bible of card magic, even though it was written to teach people how to cheat at cards. Someday I'll read it. I don't do great with books.

I've been coming to Donna's Den of Magic and Mystery for six years now, ever since I got a magic kit for my tenth birthday. The store hasn't changed much. It's long and narrow, with framed newspaper articles and signed photos of famous magicians decorating the wall space between display cabinets. Hardwood floors and a warm, dusty smell. A small stage at the back where we practice on Sundays and hang out.

I try to catch Donna's eye, but she's still on the phone. The doorbells jingle. I groan. Why now? I haven't had the chance to ask Donna about sponsoring me yet.

I turn to see who's come in.

It's Zoe. Her eyes widen when she sees me, but she recovers quickly. "How's the hand?"

I hold it out so she can see the bandage.

"Good, thanks. I was just coming to get some tips from Donna on not mutilating myself during a show."

Zoe smiles.

Donna's off the phone now, striding across the store toward us. She always walks like she's on a stage.

I introduce them.

"Alex, have you told her about the Sunday group?" Donna asks.

"Uh, no, I—"

Donna *tsks* the way Mom would if I'd forgotten to offer a guest a drink. The phone rings again, and she makes a face at it. "Tell her about the group and show her around the store. Zoe, if there's anything I can help you with, just let me know. It's a pleasure to meet you."

"Curses. Foiled again," I mutter.

"What's wrong?" Zoe asks.

"Nothing. Don't worry about it." I force a smile. "Where do you want to start? Close-up, parlor or stage?" The store is divided into three main sections. Close-up magic is stuff you can carry with you, stuff you do right in front of people, live and personal. Cards and coins, that sort of thing.

16

Parlor is stuff you'd do for a small group, maybe at a birthday party. Stuff that can be seen across a room. And stage magic is what makes up the big shows—illusions and effects that use large furniture-sized props.

"Close-up," she says.

"Cool. What kind of cards do you like?" I walk Zoe over to the close-up props and show her the Executives that I like to use, and then there's an awkward pause. My first impulse is to pull a coin out from behind her ear to make her laugh, but I can't palm it with my hand bandaged. I'm useless without magic to distract people from how useless I am.

"Is your hand going to be all right?" Zoe asks.

I nod. "There's some nerve damage, but it should be okay in a few weeks."

She flinches. "As long as it's going to get better. You know, probably if you get back to doing magic, it will help. In some hospitals they teach magic to help people get their mobility back. Like physiotherapy." Her face turns red. "I'm babbling, aren't I?"

I like that she's nervous too. She looks cute when she's nervous. I don't like that her comment just reminded me of Dad. "You're new here, right? Where did you live before?"

"I've always lived in Vancouver, but I was at school in Winnipeg the last few years."

"Why Winnipeg?"

"Good school." Her face closes.

I wait, but she doesn't explain. I reach for the cards in my back pocket, then remember that there's not much I can do with them right now. "It's great that you do magic. I've never had a magician as an assistant before."

She stiffens. "Volunteer, not assistant. I was an audience volunteer."

Donna finds us before I can put my foot any deeper into my mouth. "How's it going?"

"I love this place," Zoe says, winning a smile from Donna.

They chat. My brain is buzzing. I need to get Donna alone, away from Zoe. "Could I talk to you, just for a second?"

The phone rings again.

"Don't!" I say.

Donna lifts an eyebrow.

There's something my old softball coach used to say: *What will you do to win?* "Just—please.

There's something I want to ask you." Donna's annoyed now. Zoe's listening. My timing couldn't be worse.

Holding my gaze, Donna reaches for the phone and lifts it to her ear. "Donna's Den of Magic and Mystery." There's a pause. "Jack. Can I call you right back? Great. Thanks." She clicks the End button and slowly places the phone back on the counter, never breaking eye contact with me. "You have my attention."

"That's—thanks." Now the words swell up in my throat. I can feel Zoe watching, caught between us. "You know the Silver Stage competition."

Donna nods.

"I was wondering...would you...sponsor me?"

She sighs. "I thought that was it. Callum asked me the week before last."

"Oh."

She studies me. "Alex, it's not first-come-first-serve. I'm going to tell you what I told him. There are too many talented young magicians using this store as a home base for me to pick just one. It would be bad for business."

"So you won't sponsor either of us?" I don't know any other magicians who belong to the

Silver Stage. Not well enough to ask them, anyhow.

She picks up a poster from a pile on the counter. "These just came in."

I study the poster. I know the face looking back at me. Everybody knows that face. "Bayard Bellini?"

Despite the doofy name, Bellini's big-time. Not just in Vancouver either. He has his own television special, *Magic on the Menu.* He'll pop in on some five-star restaurant somewhere in the world and prepare a gourmet meal as the "Magic Chef Special," then wander from table to table doing close-up stuff for the ladies. Making their diamond bracelets disappear and then reappear in the pudding—that kind of thing. He has this bad-boy rock-star look going, and you see him on magazine covers at the grocery store.

"I'm holding a contest," Donna says. "He'll be the judge, and he'll sponsor the winner. Sound fair?"

Bellini as a sponsor? That's huge. I nod like a bobblehead doll.

It will come down to me or Callum Lee, like always. I'll just have to beat him this time. "When?"

She taps the poster. "Two weeks. Can you have your hand working by then?"

"Absolutely." Whatever it takes.

Zoe asks what we're talking about, so Donna and I take turns explaining about the Silver Stage Magic Competition. She looks interested but doesn't say anything about entering, and secretly I'm relieved.

Callum is competition enough.

Three

onday morning, Mrs. Forsythe looks up from her marking when I shuffle into English class. She has this ability to completely inventory a person with a glance. She nods at my hand—no more giant bandage, just gauze over the stitches now—and then spears me with her eyes.

"Mr. Eisen. Your friend Mr. Basri may take notes for you this morning." She insists on calling us all by our last names. It's weird to hear Hakim called Mr. Basri; to me, Mr. Basri is his dad.

"Thanks," I mumble. It's been a morning of stares and whispers. Anyone who wasn't actually at the talent show Friday night has heard about it by now. I slink to my seat beside Hakim.

There's a reminder on the board about next Monday's content quiz on *The Great Gatsby*. My stomach sinks. I was happy when Mrs. Forsythe handed *Gatsby* out, because it wasn't that thick a book, and it sounded like it might be about baseball or something. No such luck.

Everyone is reading silently—the start-of-class routine. I hate reading in class. To really read, I use a ruler under the line I'm on, and I track the words with my finger. It takes me about three years to finish a sentence. For in-class reading time, I just stare at the book and turn a page every now and then.

Anyhow, Hakim and I have a standing trade—he helps me through English, I teach him magic tricks.

"What happened?" Hakim whispers.

I frown to show that I don't know what he means.

"I had my hand up," he says. "Didn't you see me?"

"I saw," I mutter.

"But you thought you'd pick the girl instead? And then impress her by bleeding on her?"

"Shut up!"

"Mr. Eisen, Mr. Basri, is there something you'd like to share with the class?"

"No, ma'am," Hakim says.

I shake my head.

"Sometimes you're an idiot," Hakim whispers.

I nod.

After ten minutes, Mrs. Forsythe starts the lesson: *Who was Jay Gatsby?*

I start planning my new routine for the competition. And count the seconds until lunchtime.

* * *

In the cafeteria, I work on my back-palm, over and over. "My finger won't do what it's supposed to," I complain to Hakim.

"I thought we were *supposed* to be talking about *The Great Gatsby*. You know, so you don't flunk English."

"We will. I just want to get this working."

"So multitask. Who's the narrator? Do you remember?"

Zoe carries a tray over to our table. "Is this seat taken?" She's joined us once or twice before.

Hakim nearly falls over, pulling a chair out for her. From the look on his face, I'm pretty sure he's forgotten about *Gatsby*.

Zoe and I talk while Hakim drools. She wants to know more about the competition, so I tell her. "You should come watch. Hakim will be there. Right, Hakim?"

"Huh?"

"The competition. Saturday. At the store. You coming?"

He shakes his head. "Softball."

I turn back to Zoe. "Anyhow, you'd probably have a good time. I'll introduce you around, and you can cheer me on. Think you can make it?"

Her face turns red. "I just remembered I have math homework. See you guys around!"

* * *

I show up at Donna's an hour early for the contest. Nobody from my family is with me, although Mom seems to feel that her not being at my last show had something to do with me spiking my hand, so she's coming later.

Inside the store, I take one of the seats Donna has set up in front of the stage. I check the equipment in my backpack and go through my new routine in my head. Again. And again. It's bad to be doing something untested for a contest this important, but I feel like my Weird Science routine is jinxed.

Donna's whisking around the store in her leopard-print dress, making sure everything is ready. She squeezes my shoulder. "Just relax and have fun with it. You'll knock 'em dead." She pauses and looks more closely at me. "Alex. Calm down. You're going to be fine."

I'm calm. Or I would be if I could remember how to breathe.

I work my hand. The stitches are gone, but the finger is still a bit stiff, and I can't feel much along one side of it.

I pace the store, pausing to rub the silver frame for luck.

Callum shows up wearing a tux. *Goof.* He sees me and scowls. "Nice show the other week."

"Yeah, well, at least I'm not dressed like a trained monkey."

He flicks an imaginary speck of dust off his collar and stands up straight so he's taller than me.

A few minutes later Bayard Bellini shows up, also in a tux; of course, the top buttons and bow tie are undone for his usual just-rolled-out-of-bed-with-three-hot-ladies look. There's some old guy with him, wearing a long, wrinkled brown coat and a two-day beard. Something about him is familiar.

Donna doesn't look too pleased to see the old guy. She pulls him aside.

I start walking toward Bayard, but Callum gets there first, and they start joking about their matching suits, making like they're long-lost twins, except for Callum being Asian. Callum undoes his bow tie to match Bayard's.

I close my eyes and press my forehead against a metal DVD rack. It's cool against my sweaty skin.

I feel a hand on my shoulder. A lighter touch than Donna's. "Are you all right?"

Zoe. I turn to face her. She looks great. Dressed in black, loose hair, shiny lips. I've never been so happy to see anyone in my life. "You came!" Impulsively, I hug her.

She stiffens.

I let go. "Sorry." *Stupid. Stupid, stupid, stupid.*

Her face softens. "It's all right. Alex, there's something I need to tell you."

Donna nudges us out of the way and leans a glittery board up against a display case. It has the order of contestants on it. My mouth dries up when I see that I'm going first. Callum is last.

Zoe's staring at the board too, and that's when I see it. Her name. Going third.

She isn't here to support me. She's the competition.

"I know I should have told you sooner, but I was nervous. I've never competed before, and—"

I tune her out. There's a roaring in my ears.

I told her about the contest, told her how much it meant to me. Every single day we saw each other in chemistry class. Not once did she mention that she was planning to compete against me.

I step away from her and bang into a stand of cheap gag tricks. It falls slowly, and I have a second of thinking I can catch it before I overbalance. The crash has everyone staring at me there on the floor on my butt. Zoe. Donna. The old guy. Callum.

Bayard Bellini.

Callum laughs. "Nice."

Zoe tries to help me, but I ignore her hand and get up on my own. I breathe hard through my nose as Donna comes over, and we right the display together.

"Why don't you go get ready?" she suggests quietly.

"I'm ready."

"Where's your lab coat?"

"New routine."

Donna frowns. She opens her mouth, then closes it again and shakes her head slightly. She pats me on the shoulder. "Break a leg."

I find a quiet corner of the store and lean against the wall, eyes closed.

I won't let myself be distracted anymore.

I'm here to win.

Four

onna's at the microphone, welcoming everyone. Her voice echoes in my head. People applaud. I clap my sweaty hands together once, twice. Five heartbeats for each clap.

And now she's saying my name. I raise my chin and force my shoulders down. Smile at the audience like I mean it. Donna set out thirty chairs, and they're all full, with some overflow. Mom snuck into the store late. She waves from a back corner.

I check the seat I rigged, to see who's in it.

Callum. Of course it's Callum. Because the universe hates me.

I shake my arms twice and crack my neck, breathing out, and then take a few running steps onto the stage. Eight minutes for my routine. Eight minutes until I can disappear.

I produce a quarter from thin air. My patter was supposed to be about luck. Looking at Zoe, I change my mind. It's called a loyal-coin routine, after all. "I want to talk to you about loyalty. What does loyalty mean to you? To me, it means that someone is there for you." I vanish the coin. "Even when you can't see them."

Donna, standing beside the stage, looks worried.

"Donna, could you please pass me that Sharpie from your desk? The magic marker?" My stress on the word *magic* falls flat, because I didn't start funny.

I use the magic marker as a wand to make the quarter reappear in my closed right hand. It's a simple trick and gets a small laugh. "This must be my lucky coin after all." Oops. I didn't start out talking about luck. "I mean, it's very loyal."

Mom claps a few times, but no one else does. And then, just as Mom stops, Zoe and Donna start, then fade out quickly. Awkward.

Bayard Bellini yawns from the front row. Beside him, the old man in the brown coat snorts and glances up at the ceiling tiles.

I hold up the coin, pinched between two fingers. "But how do you know it's the same coin? Let's make sure." I step down off the stage and thrust the Sharpie and the quarter at Bayard, making him focus on me. "An autograph for a fan?" Up close, I see that he's wearing guyliner.

Smiling a showman's smile, he stands up and turns around so the audience can watch him initial the quarter. And then the quarter disappears. He pulls it from behind my ear, the way you would do at a little kid's birthday party. This time, the crowd's applause is real.

I force myself to applaud along with them.

Donna taps her watch.

I bound back onto the stage, quarter held high. "I bet it's good luck now!" I pretend to pass it through the bottom of a regular drinking glass. "See? I never used to be able to do that." There's good-natured laughter from the crowd. Even Zoe is smiling.

Not that I care.

The coin is still in the glass, which I fill with water from a pitcher on the table. "Excuse me," I say, as if my throat is dry. I drink the water,

turning slightly away from the audience. As I
drain the glass, the quarter slides into my mouth.

I grab my throat and cough, pretending to
choke on it. Some water ends up on the floor.
And then, just as Donna's looking worried and
stepping toward the stage, I secretly cough the
coin into my hand. I pound myself on the chest.
"That's—that's—I think I swallowed it," I croak.

I stand there for a moment, doing my best
to look lost. The old man beside Bayard leans
forward, studying me. I start checking all my
pockets, as if looking for inspiration. Mid pat-
down, I drop the quarter through a hole in a
pocket and feel it fall along my leg, into my open-
laced sneaker. Perfect.

The audience is starting to shift and murmur.
Bayard looks bored.

Not perfect.

I pull the deck of Executives from the back
pocket of my jeans, pretending I've just realized
it's there. "But, um, when your friends desert
you—or you accidentally swallow them—it's good
to have a backup plan." I do some of the same cuts
and flourishes that worked for the talent show,

but I fumble one of the cuts when my finger doesn't cooperate.

Zoe's biting her lip. The look on her face—real worry, real concern—almost throws me. Then I remember why she's here.

I choose a friendly face in the audience—Paul, a thirteen-year-old who's been coming to Donna's for almost two years now. He picks a card from my deck, apparently at random, but I force the ace of clubs, my favorite card. Paul shows the rest of the crowd his card while I turn away. With my back to the audience, I massage my sore hand.

Paul slides his card into the middle of the deck. I start to shuffle, promising the audience that Paul's card will rise to the top.

Finally, I flip up the top card. The ten of hearts. "And here's your card!"

Paul's face falls. "That wasn't it."

Callum coughs into his fist. It sounds a lot like "loser."

I hold up a hand. "Wait! I can fix this." I squeeze my eyes shut, pretending to concentrate. Then I focus on the rigged seat in the audience.

Callum's seat.

But I don't have a way around it. My brain's spinning too fast to come up with a save. "Callum, could you please check under your seat?"

With a sneer, Callum gropes under his chair, and then he holds up his hands for everyone to see. "Much like your act, I come up empty."

"Don't be a jerk," Paul says.

"Check again." My teeth are clenched.

Donna glares at Callum. He fishes out the ace of clubs, secured by double-stick tape. He holds the card up for a split second before letting it flutter to the floor. "Ooooops."

There's no applause. I'm sweating. I start patting my pockets again, mumbling something about missing my lucky coin. I start to sniff, then sneeze loudly into a red handkerchief that zips away into a flying-handkerchief routine. I chase the cloth around the stage, barely gripping the edges as it flies in front of me. It's pretty much the same thing I did for the school talent show, except with no apple. "So much for loyalty," I grumble. At least that gets a laugh.

I pretend to trip and stumble across the stage. "What was that?" I examine the stage as the hand-kerchief drifts to the floor. "Something tripped me.

Something..." I'm down on all fours now, feeling my way around the stage. Then, abruptly, I stop. I face the audience and pull off my left shoe. I shake it in the air, standing up slowly. There's silence from the crowd. Finally, I have them.

I take off my right shoe.

And, of course, there's the coin. I show it to the audience. Bayard confirms that it's the one with his signature on it. This time, I don't let him steal my spotlight. Mom's clapping as if she's never seen anyone do magic before. The old guy beside Callum nods at me once, slowly. For some reason that makes me feel good.

I kiss the coin, tuck it back into my pocket and thank the audience for their applause. Still in my sock feet, I bow. And then I escape from the stage.

I'd give anything to go back and do it all again, do it better.

I take Paul's seat as he heads to the stage. Someone reaches from behind to tap my shoulder and give me a thumbs-up. I smile automatically.

I laugh when I hear laughter, clap when I hear applause. Nothing registers. My act replays over and over in my head. Suddenly Paul's done, and Zoe's up.

Zoe doesn't talk; she has classical music playing instead. She starts with a cups-and-ball routine. She's fast—not perfect, but fast. At one point she has the sponge ball "transform" into a crumpled card, and she smooths the card until it looks just like new, which is a nice transition into her card tricks. The actual tricks are pretty basic, but her presentation is good. She ends with ninja rings, the miniature version of those linking rings that stage magicians use. She has five of them, and her technique is solid. She slips the rings into and out of one another, and the illusion holds every time. Again, she sticks with the basics, but the way she moves around the stage with the rings, jumping and twirling and pointing her toes, it's almost like a dance routine. By the time she bows, she hasn't said one word to the audience, but the applause for her lasts longer than it did for me or Paul.

After Zoe there's someone else, and after that person someone else. I know these kids. Some of them are my friends. I try to watch. My ears are ringing. I keep seeing Zoe whirl around the stage, and I keep hearing myself fumble my lines.

By the time Callum is up, I can breathe again. I want his act to pass in a blur like all the others, but it doesn't. He's good. He's up there in his stupid monkey suit, making cheesy jokes, charming the audience. The kicker is when he needs a volunteer and calls up Bayard. And Bayard actually agrees and goes along with the stupid choose-a-card-any-card routine.

Before Callum's final, overly theatrical bow is over, I know. I make small talk with everyone while Bayard confers with Donna—and the old guy, for some reason—but we all know it's a formality. Callum kicked butt today. He kicked my butt.

He deserves the win.

"Alex, you were great!" Mom swoops in for a hug.

"No, I wasn't," I say. "But thanks anyhow."

Before Mom can say anything else, Donna takes the stage. She's added a top hat to her crazy outfit. "Congratulations, everyone." She waits as people fumble to their seats. "Thanks for coming, and thank you all for your support of the store. One of the best parts of my job is getting to know all these fabulous young magicians. Let's give them all another round of applause."

I want her to get it over with. Even though I know I lost, there's some small, stupid part of me that doesn't. That hopeful part is making my palms sweat and my knees jitter, and I need to stop it or it's only going to be worse when I come in second to Callum.

It *always* comes down to me or Callum, and today he was amazing.

"They didn't make it easy for the judges today, did they?" Donna continues. "But as most of you know, what's at stake here is the sponsorship of the one and only Bayard Bellini." Bayard stands and bows. "There can be only one winner, and so we had to make a tough choice." Her eyes skate past me, and a thread of ice unspools itself from the base of my spine and slides up my back.

Donna takes off her top hat and shows that it's empty, then pulls a slip of paper from inside it. "Second runner-up," she says. "Alex Eisen."

Five

Second runner-up? That's third place. Not even second. Someone has hollowed out my insides.

Paul nudges me. "Hey, man, congrats! Go on, get up there!"

Somehow I wobble my way to the stage. I shake hands with Donna and with Bayard and accept the certificate they hand to me. I force a smile and mumble my thanks. Donna motions for me to stay on the stage, at the back.

So I have a perfect view as she calls Zoe as first runner-up. Zoe comes to stand beside me. Her back is straighter than a brand-new deck of cards. And then—the moment we've all been waiting for—Callum Lee wins first prize. In addition to getting a nice, shiny trophy, he'll be sponsored by Bayard Bellini to compete in the Silver Stage Magic Competition at the regional level.

I want to throw up.

"Careful," Zoe whispers to me. That's when I realize I'm crumpling my certificate. "Are you all right?"

"Never better."

Mom offers me a ride home, but I'm not ready to leave. Once I walk out of this store, it's really over; as long as I'm here, someone might run up to me and say it's all been a terrible mistake. So I say goodbye to her and move like a zombie through the thinning crowd, saying thanks and congratulations.

Bayard and Callum disappear through the front door together, probably to tell each other how awesome they are.

Soon most people have cleared out. The rumpled old man who was beside Bayard is sitting on one corner of the stage. Zoe and Paul and a couple of other kids have pulled chairs into a circle around him. He seems to be showing them card handling.

I make my way to Donna, by the cash register. "I wanted to say thanks. For today," I start.

"It didn't work out like I wanted, but it was still a cool thing you did, bringing Bayard Bellini out to see us."

"He and Callum have gone to discuss details." She brushes some dust off the counter, but I know she's watching my reaction.

"Callum was good today."

She nods. "He was also a class-A jerk. I'll have a word with him about that."

I shrug as if it doesn't matter.

"We all have bad days, Alex," she says. "I'm sorry that yours was today."

"Me too."

"You should go join the others. Jack doesn't teach very often. I'm surprised he's doing it now." Her expression as she looks at the stage is approving but guarded.

"Jack?"

She raises an eyebrow. "You don't recognize him? Jack Spader. The Jack of Spades."

That must be why he looked familiar. He wrote my favorite book on card magic—one of the only ones I've actually read. Donna always has it on display at the counter. I can't believe this is the same guy. "That's him? Seriously?"

"I kid you not." She busies herself with the cash register. "I'd know—he's my father. Taught me my first card trick before I could write my name."

"Seriously?"

She smiles at me.

Jack Spader is Donna's dad. How cool is that? I turn back to the stage.

Paul makes room for me. Jack demonstrates a hold, and the others all copy. He studies their hands, making adjustments. I pull my own deck out of my back pocket and give it a try.

When he reaches me, he grunts. "Sloppy. You're broadcasting." He adjusts the angle of my hand and moves my fingers farther apart. The movement stretches my scar. I wince.

"What did you do to your hand, kid?"

My face heats up. "Nothing."

Jack moves on. "And then, once you've got the hold, your double lift looks like this." He flips two cards as one. It's incredibly smooth. "It ain't fancy, but it finishes clean. That's what you want."

Once we've mastered that one, Jack shows us a new shuffle that keeps a card on the bottom of the deck. It looks like he's mixing the cards properly, but again and again he shows us—the jack of spades is always there. "Bottom dweller, he is," Jack says.

None of us laugh. We're too busy trying to copy the shuffle.

Finally, Donna emerges from her office. "Hate to break up the party, folks, but it's closing time. Jack, you need a lift?"

"Much obliged."

I hang back while Paul and the other kids leave, hoping to catch Donna alone. Zoe doesn't seem to be in any hurry to leave either. I drag my feet to the front of the store, hoping she'll get ahead of me. No luck. I get the feeling she's waiting for a chance to talk to me.

Donna sweeps up to me. If I don't ask now, when will I? "Donna, about the sponsorship—"

Her face stiffens. "I know how much this means to you, Alex, but I've already told you why I can't sponsor anyone. That's what today was about." She glances at Jack.

Jack studies me, eyes narrowed. "Tell me. That routine you did—did you throw it together last night?"

It's close enough to the truth that I look away.

"Newsflash, kid. You can't phone it in and expect to win. Show me what you can really do."

"Do your routine," Donna says. "The science one." She says it like it matters, like she wants me to impress him.

I swallow. "Pretend I'm wearing a lab coat," I tell Jack, making my way to the stage.

I do the parts of the routine I can do with the props I have, while Jack, Donna and Zoe watch. It's nearly flawless. It's the show I should have done for Bayard.

When I'm finished, Jack jerks a thumb at Zoe. "You two get along?"

I look away. Neither of us answers.

He grunts. "That's too bad. I might have taken you on, if you came as a set."

Donna's eyes widen.

"What do you mean?" Zoe asks.

"What I mean is, you move well, and you're pretty enough, but your magic is still basic. We can work on that; it just takes time. You've got stage sense. This one, when he's paying attention, can pull off the hard stuff that the judges will like—but he's sloppy, and he talks too much.

Between the two of you, you might have some-thing." He shrugs.

"We'll do it." The words fly out before my brain okays them.

Zoe glares at me. "You don't speak for me."

"Tell you what," Jack says. "Mondays and Wednesdays I teach poker at a restaurant on Main called Houdini's Hideout. You swing by after school Monday if you're interested, and we'll draw up a contract."

Donna's frowning. "You're still doing that?"

"Gotta pay rent," he growls.

"We'll be there," I promise.

At the same time, Zoe says, "I'll think about it."

Jack shrugs. "No skin off my back."

I don't want to work with Zoe. I don't want to work with anyone. But it's a chance to compete. Right now, it's my only chance.

All I have to do is convince Zoe.

Six

There's not a lot going right today. I'm pretty sure I flunked the *Gatsby* quiz we had in English, and my chemistry lab experiment flopped. Now I have to make nice with Zoe and convince her to work with me and Jack.

I shove my way through the post-bell rush and catch Zoe at her locker.

"He called me pretty," she says.

"So?"

"I'm not stage dressing, Alex. I want to be up there as a magician or not at all. And I know how these things work." She slams the locker door. "If you have a boy-girl act, guess which one is going to be the assistant?"

I'd kind of assumed it would be her, but something tells me not to say that. "Lots of magicians work as teams. Penn and Teller. Siegfried and Roy."

"Abbott and Costello." She starts walking.

"Yeah!" Wait. "No. Were they magicians?"

She sighs. It's the Alex-is-an-idiot sigh.

I hate that she's making me do this. I don't even want to team up with her—I'm being forced into this as much as she is. I shouldn't have to beg for the honor.

What will you do to win?

"Besides, he didn't just say you were pretty. He said you moved well, remember? And you beat me."

She makes eye contact for the first time.

"If you don't want to do this, why did you even bother competing at Donna's?"

She pushes past me, headed for the front door.

I get in front of her. "I'm serious, Zoe. Why?"

"I wanted to see—" She stops.

"To see what? If you could beat me?"

"None of your business." Her head is down so I can't see her face.

"I'm going," I call after her. "I'm going to meet him with or without you. This is a huge chance, Zoe. You're crazy to let it go."

Hakim sidles up beside me, shaking his head. "Dude. Desperation. Not cool."

* * *

Houdini's Hideout is two blocks from my favorite comic-book store. It's not the worst part of town, but there are a few closed storefronts around, and graffiti in the alleys.

I lock my bike outside and step into the restaurant. A bar runs across the back wall, and round tables are scattered throughout the room. My runners stick to the hardwood floors.

Jack's at a table, playing cards with four younger men. I move toward them, squeezing past a woman reading a newspaper. There's no sign of Zoe, and I let myself hope a little. Jack wanted a team, but if she were ready to compete, she'd be here. Maybe he'll agree to take me on. Just me. No partner.

When I get close, Jack signals me to wait. I sit nearby and angle my chair to watch.

The bartender comes over and I order a Coke. I stick it on a cardboard coaster and wait, shuffling my cards and practicing the grip Jack showed me.

The door opens, a crack of sunlight slicing into the dim room. It's Zoe. I fumble my cards, spilling them across the table.

She stands in the doorway for a moment, looking at Jack playing cards at his table and me sitting alone at mine. I don't signal her, don't do anything to make it easy. Finally she joins me.

"What's going on?" she asks, resting her elbows on the table while I clean up my cards. "Why isn't he with you?"

Something's wrestling inside of me. She's here, so it's all going to happen now. We're at the start of something, a roller coaster about to climb. But earlier, when she said she wasn't coming, I let myself believe for a second that I might be taking that ride alone. "You're late" is all I manage to spit out.

Now that she's here, Jack excuses himself from the card game and takes the seat beside me, across from Zoe. Like I wasn't worth his time when it was just me. "So we're agreed, are we?"

"I want to hear what you have in mind," Zoe says.

He nods slowly. "Fair enough. All right, here it is. We design an act that features the two of you and balances your strengths and weaknesses. I sponsor you to enter the competition. You win."

"We win?" I ask. He says it like it's a done deal.

"That's what I said. You win. I take fifty percent."

I don't mind splitting the winnings. For me, this isn't about the money.

"And if we lose?" Zoe asks.

He shrugs. "It's a gamble, I suppose." His eyes gleam. "Do as I say and you won't lose."

"Where do I sign?" I ask, ignoring Zoe.

"There's an idea." Jack grabs a clean paper napkin from a neighboring table and, with a flourish, produces a pen. He spreads the napkin out flat. "I will do what Jack says," he mumbles as he writes.

"A contract on a napkin? Seriously?" Zoe asks, frowning.

"It's the signatures that matter." He signs his name at the bottom. The napkin tears a little.

Zoe pins Jack with her eyes. "I'm not here to be a magician's assistant. Are we clear on that?"

"What makes you think you're going to be the assistant?" he asks.

"I'm female. You said I was pretty." Her cheeks color.

"I see." Jack nods slowly. "You are pretty. Oh, don't worry; you're a few decades too young for my taste. But pretty will help with the judges. This one here, he's not so pretty." He studies me. I force myself to stare back and take a slow sip of my drink. "What say we make him the assistant?"

Coke comes out my nose. "What?"

He scoots his chair away from me. Zoe hands me a napkin. Not the contract one.

"Try not to do that on stage," Jack says, deadpan.

"Why should I be the assistant? Why do we even have to do it that way?"

"Calm down. I'm not going to stick you in tights. But you're going to play a supporting role for a bit. Learn to read the audience and watch your angles. Stay on track—you get into trouble when you start ad-libbing."

This isn't what I signed up for.

Actually, I haven't signed up for anything yet. I shake my head and throw money on the table to cover my drink. "Thanks anyhow. I'm in this to do magic, not to watch it."

"Alex—" Zoe starts.

I hold up my hands. "No, it's cool. Good luck. Break a leg or whatever."

She looks sick.

On my way out, I pass the newspaper-reading lady. It's one of the local papers, and she's holding it so that I can see the front page. Which shows a picture of Bayard and Callum, wearing their matching tuxes.

I freeze. *What will you do to win?*

That's when I know I'll do whatever Jack tells me. Whatever it takes. I don't want to be Zoe's assistant, but Jack saw me on an off day. I'll prove that I deserve the lead.

I turn and walk back to Jack and Zoe. The napkin-contract and pen are still on the table. I grab the pen and sign, tearing the paper. "I'm in." It comes out as a snarl.

Zoe's eyes are wide. She signs after me, more carefully.

Jack takes the napkin and folds it. It disappears with a flourish of his hands and instead he's holding a playing card—the jack of spades, of course—with an address scrawled across it in marker. He hands it to me. "Be at this address at four o'clock tomorrow, both of you. Now if you'll excuse me, I have a game to win."

He rejoins the poker game, leaving Zoe and me looking at each other.

Seven

The next day, when Zoe and I get to the address Jack gave us, I'm surprised to see that it's a storage garage, one of those rent-by-the-month things. "You think this is it?" I ask.

She knocks on the blue garage door.

It slides up and Jack waves us in. It's a corner unit, a bit wider than the others, lit by fluorescent bulbs. Inside, near the front, he has a threadbare couch and some lumpy armchairs set up almost like a living room. It smells musty.

Not where I imagined us practicing magic. "This isn't where you live, is it?"

He follows us in as the garage door closes. "Not this week."

I can't tell if he's joking.

Zoe has already moved past me to a section of wall that's covered by an assortment of mirrors. Some are framed, some not; most of them are cracked or chipped. It's like a crazy person's dressing room. She faces herself and runs a finger along a crack.

"Careful," I say.

She steps back and smiles, striking a dance pose with curved arms. "It's a studio."

"You got it," Jack says, sounding pleased. That's when I notice the masking tape laid out on the floor in the shape of a stage, facing the mirrors.

"Cool," I say, but I'm annoyed that Zoe scored the point. Jack stands still, watching us explore.

I walk past the makeshift stage, trying not to notice my scattered reflections. They're disorienting and a bit eerie. Still, I get where Jack is going with the setup. Practicing in front of mirrors is the only way to see what the audience sees.

Something white flutters, catching my eye. It's our napkin-contract, taped to the wall.

At the back of the garage there's a workshop area—power tools and lumber. The smell of cut wood masks the garage's mustiness. It looks like

Jack's been building props. I see a box for sawing someone in half that's nearly finished, and two tables with secret compartments waiting to be stained. I flip the compartment on one of the tables. "Smooth. You should get Donna to carry these in her store."

"She knows where to find me if she needs anything." There's a wall in his voice. "Let's get to work."

Jack takes one of the armchairs. Zoe and I sit on either end of the couch. Her nose wrinkles. A steel storage trunk squats like a coffee table between the chairs and the couch. It looks like something out of World War II. A space heater hums nearby.

"Cards away, champ," Jack says.

I hadn't even noticed that I'd taken them out and was riffling them—flexing up a corner and letting the cards slide past my thumb and flap back into place. Dad calls it "snapping" the cards, and he's always on my case about it, but it does help break in a deck. Mostly, though, my hands just like having cards in them.

Jack nods as I place my deck on the trunk. "That's something I noticed in your routine—a lot of unnecessary movement and card handling. You're riffling and dribbling all the time those cards are in your hands. By the time you get to the effect, the audience has been watching your cards jump around so long, they don't know where to look. Basically, if you're in a performance space, don't pull it out unless you're going to shoot it." He looks around the garage. "For us, for now, this is a performance space."

I lean forward so he'll see that I'm ready to learn. "Where do we start?"

Jack scratches behind one ear. "Well, you're both under seventeen, right?"

Zoe and I nod.

"That puts you in the youth category, which is good, because it means anything goes. Close-up. Stage magic. A mix."

"Close-up," I say. No brainer.

He points at me. "Think bigger. The winning close-up routines these days are using parlor-type effects. Even if you do close-up, you have to make it play big. Like this." He spreads my cards across the trunk, making the spread stretch nearly from one side to the other. "Do you see how that's more visible?"

We take turns trying the spread. It's wider than I'm used to, but I catch on faster than Zoe does.

"Whatever you're doing, think presentation," Jack says. "It's not what you do, it's what the judges see that counts. Keep your visual moments big and your sleights hidden."

"Got it," I say, nodding.

Zoe's taking notes. *Keener.*

"Now. Let's talk about a routine," Jack says.

"How does it work? Do we combine our acts?" Zoe asks.

"Slap two mishmash routines together, you get mush. No, we start fresh. A good routine tells a story. You can thank Copperfield for that. So before we talk tricks, we figure out your story. Give me some themes."

"Weird science," I say.

Zoe glares at me. "New themes. Ones that haven't already been done, starring you."

I shrug. "It's a good theme."

"Just try for a one-word idea for now," Jack says. "Love."

"Hate," Zoe says.

"War," I say.

"Peace," Zoe says.

"You say up, she says down. I didn't ask for opposites, I asked for a theme," Jack says. "We'll start with mine, then. Love. You're a boy-girl team; there's got to be some way to use that to our advantage."

I groan.

Jack shoots me a sharp look. "Which reminds me, no dating for you two. Not as long as we're working together. I don't need the drama."

"We're not—" I say.

"I would never—" Zoe says.

Ouch.

Jack tells us to write down our ideas for a routine about love. Tricks, props, storylines— anything. Zoe has to lend me a piece of paper and a pen. I write slowly, making the words thick and heavy, using my arm to hide the paper from view so Jack can't see my lousy spelling.

By the time we're done, our combined lists cover flower tricks, phone-number tricks, wedding-ring tricks and card tricks featuring the queen of hearts. I've put the king of hearts on my list, but Jack points out that he has a sword through his head. Not romantic.

Zoe has come up with the idea of a dinner date as a setting for tricks like floating napkins and bending spoons. I wish I'd thought of that.

Jack nods. "We can work with that. Boy meets girl, boy loses girl..."

"Why not girl meets boy?" Zoe asks.

"Boy and girl meet each other," Jack says. "There's interest, maybe you come on stage separately, and at first things are good. Then there's a fight of some kind. A disagreement. You two should be good at that part. And then we find a way to resolve things in the end."

"Happily ever after." I'm using what Mom calls my snark voice. "Why does it have to be a love story?"

"Because the judges will like it," Jack says. "You want to win, right? Magic isn't about you. It's about the audience."

So there it is. I can win as part of a two-person love-story team or stick to my guns and lose my chance to compete. *What will you do to win?* "Fine," I say. "Boy meets girl meets boy. Now what?"

"Now we break it down. What might a story like that look like on the stage?"

"Aren't we going to do any actual magic today?" The words are out before I can stop them.

Jack studies me, face blank, but I think I see a hint of disappointment in his eyes. "We can do that," he says finally. "We don't know specific tricks yet, but we'll work on general technique. Your homework is to draft a two-person routine around the story we talked about."

So we work on card handling. These are all things I've done before, but Jack has ways of doing them, of positioning my hands and fingers, that are better. Smoother. Cleaner. It's exciting.

"A larger action covers a smaller one," he tells me.

"Dai Vernon," I answer.

He smiles. "Very good. One of the greatest magicians who ever lived."

Zoe looks uncertain. She's struggling with her ambitious card routine; a lot of what Jack is showing us seems to be new to her. She needs help with technique. She's good at pulling out the visual moments, though, and keeping her movements clean. Jack praises her presentation.

One thing I'll say for Zoe: She knows how to do the work. When she gets something wrong, she listens to the correction and then does it over and over again until she gets it right.

For me, the focus is on what Jack calls "stage smarts." Part of that is the unnecessary card handling. "It's your default," Jack explains again. "But it distracts the audience. You control the cards; they don't control you." The trouble is, half the time I don't notice I'm doing it. And even when I'm not shuffling the cards, I'm moving too much. Taking steps, bouncing my knees, fidgeting.

Zoe doesn't fidget.

Our time is up before I know it. Jack sets our practice schedule—Tuesdays and Thursdays after school, plus all day Saturday whenever we can. Dad's going to flip. I'll just have to keep my grades up. Do better. Give him no reason to kick up a fuss about how I spend my time.

"You're really good," Zoe says as we wait for the bus.

It feels like a peace offering. "So are you," I say. "I've been doing magic for longer is all."

I don't like the love story idea. I'm still worried about playing backup to Zoe, even though I think I impressed Jack today. We don't know what tricks we're doing yet, but I feel good. I feel like I leveled up just being here.

For the first time, I think maybe this can work.

Eight

Wednesday, Mrs. Forsythe assigns a paper on *The Great Gatsby*. Which I still haven't read.

Hakim claps me on the shoulder. "I'll help you. It'll be okay."

But it won't, because I have a ton of work in my other subjects, and it's already all I can do to carve out time for magic practice. Zoe and I have our assigned times with Jack, but I figure I need to be doing at least an hour a day to stay sharp. If I lose my edge, I'll never win the lead back from Zoe.

At lunch, my cards come out of my pocket as soon as we sit down.

"Choose a card," I tell Hakim.

He rolls his eyes but does it.

I go through the steps, having him stick the card in the middle of the deck and then finding it again. It's something we've done a million times. Even Hakim knows how to do this one. But this time he looks at me sharply when I produce his nine of clubs.

"You did something different," he says. "Not the key card, like you taught me. This way is better."

It's the same. I did the same trick. And even though he knows how it's done, he didn't spot it.

He makes me do the trick again, slower. I don't usually repeat tricks. The first time you show a trick, they're watching the effect. The second time, they're watching to see how it's done. For Hakim, though, I will. That's part of our deal, in exchange for his help with English.

He watches closely. And I still fool him.

"You're getting better at this," he says.

"Jack's a good teacher." As I say the words, I realize something: Jack's not just my ticket into this competition; he's the guy who's going to teach me what I need to make it as a magician. So if I don't want to end up playing backup to

Zoe O'Neill..."I need Zoe to quit," I tell Hakim. "And if I want to keep Jack on my side, it has to be her idea."

"And she's just going to give up because you want her to? I thought the whole point of magicians was that you're the kids who don't give up. You know—that's why you can actually do the card tricks, and I just know how they work."

He has a point. I shrug anyhow. "I have to try."

"Just don't be a jerk about it. Zoe's cool. I *like* her."

"Hakim, you know I'm not like that."

He nods. "Which is why we're friends."

"I won't do anything brutal. It won't take much. She doesn't want to work with me any more than I want to work with her."

* * *

Toward the end of Thursday's practice, we have the outline of a routine. At least, we know the main elements and sequences. The routine starts with Zoe's ninja rings, but we haven't sorted out exactly what tricks she'll be doing or for how long. After a minute or so, I come on doing some flashy card stuff, but again, we haven't picked out exactly what I'll be doing. Still, I can see how the routine is going to play.

Mostly we work separately, taking turns and using tricks we've done before, in our individual routines. I'm okay with that part. There are a few parts where we have to work together. Those are the rough bits.

They're also, Jack says, the payoff. "This is where your points are going to come from. The judges aren't stupid. They know what teen magicians can do—they've seen it before. And, forgive me saying so, you got nothing new, neither one of you. Working together, though, that's hard. That takes discipline. And the judges know it."

"So you're saying we're not that good, but if we're not that good together, we get more points for it?" Zoe's voice is flat.

Jack beams. "Exactly."

Just what I want to hear.

"Why bother with us if we're not good?" Zoe asks.

His eyes gleam. "Magic is never about what is. It's about what might be."

"So to you, we're a magic trick," I say.

"To me, you're a bet. Just like I am to you." He raps on the army-trunk coffee table.

But I think we all might have made the wrong bet. It's the working-together parts that aren't working.

The trick I hate most is when Zoe makes me disappear. It's done with a mirror and a tablecloth. The basic story is that we go on a date together, and we're supposed to be showing each other magic, but I'm being a jerk about it, not letting her have her turn. And so she makes me disappear.

It's humiliating. Plus, it means that for a full minute of our eight-minute routine, I'm crouching behind a table.

"Why do we have to do it this way?" I ask, crouched behind one of the secret-compartment tables Jack has built. In the mirror on the wall, I look like a little kid.

Jack's been watching us from the front of the stage, pacing back and forth to get different angles. "Because it's mostly a close-up routine, so the judges won't be expecting it."

"It's not like we're going to fool them."

He shakes his head. "The idea isn't to fool the judges. You're not good enough to fool them. The idea is to entertain them. And this—the guy disappearing, not the girl—is different. So it's entertaining."

Zoe's expression, split across two mirrors, is skeptical.

I make things hard for Zoe in little ways. A pass that's just a bit slow, so she has to reach and her sight lines are thrown off. A line delivered with the wrong emphasis, so it becomes my punch line, not hers. When she complains, Jack says she has to learn to deal with the unexpected.

"He's doing it on purpose," she says.

Jack nods. "Don't worry. He'll stop when he figures it out."

"When I figure what out?"

He smiles. And then we go back to working on the routine.

When our time is up and we're getting ready to leave, he calls me back. Zoe waits for me outside. "There's something I want you to remember," Jack says.

"Yeah?" I lean forward, waiting to hear whatever tip he has for me.

"I signed a two-person team," Jack says. "If you can't be part of that team, I'd like to know the reason why."

I swallow. "No reason. I can be part of the team. I will."

"See you Saturday."

* * *

A paper lands on my desk. Before I even see what it is, I see the F at the top of it.

"Not your best work, Mr. Eisen," Mrs. Forsythe says. "Do you think I can't tell when someone hasn't read the book?"

"Sorry," I mumble.

"You'll need to get this signed."

Hakim turns his quiz over quickly, but not before I see the A.

"Bad luck, bro," he whispers.

I shake my head. It wasn't luck, and we both know it.

* * *

At Saturday's practice, I have a new plan. If I can't force her out, I'll show her up.

We spend some time on the dinner-date part of the routine, figuring out what tricks we might do.

This is supposed to be a section where I'm showing off anyhow, so I crank it up a notch, going for the fancy stuff, and I barely let Zoe get a trick—or a word—in edgewise.

"Do you mind?" she asks, the third time I cut her off.

"I'm in character," I say, smiling sweetly.

"Okay, tone it down a bit," Jack says, but when I pretend to pass Zoe the salt, covered in a table napkin, and it turns out to be an empty napkin, he laughs.

At one point, when I'm hiding behind the table, Zoe's supposed to notice the cards I left on top of it. She fans them out, and the queen of hearts is reversed, back to front, so it's the only card facing the audience. It's a reveal, because earlier in the routine the audience watched me pocket that card.

Zoe's clumsy with the fan, so I seize the chance. "You know what would be cool? If you did split fans. So you open the fan and see the queen. You throw those cards away and create a new fan. The queen of hearts keeps appearing, reversed. Three times would be good."

Jack nods slowly. "That could work."

Zoe's face reddens. "Sure, if I could do it. Let me work on it, okay?"

"It's not that hard. I'll show you." I do it flawlessly. After all, I spent most of last night practicing.

"I like the effect," Jack says. "It's something we can work on. Zoe, don't worry about it for now. Let's keep going."

Every time I get the chance, I substitute a showier trick for a plainer one, a harder one for a simpler one. It becomes clear that Zoe just doesn't have as many options as I do. What she can do, she does well, but she hasn't got my repertoire. "Sorry, I thought everybody knew that one," I say after suggesting an advanced card trick.

She narrows her eyes at me.

We haven't worked out the finale yet. "Throw me some ideas," Jack says, pacing back and forth in front of the mirrors. "How can you show the audience that you've come together at the end?"

"It depends on the story," Zoe says before I can answer. "It depends why we split up in the first place. Right now, it's because he's an obnoxious, self-centered jerk. I mean, that's why I make him disappear, right? So I can't see why I—I mean, my character—would want anything to do with him."

"Maybe your character needs to learn to take a joke," I fire back.

"Maybe the joke needs to be funny."

Jack holds up his hands. "Save the drama for the stage."

"What if I don't bring him back?" Zoe asks, stepping in front of me. "Seriously. If we move the disappearance closer to the end of the routine, it starts and finishes with me alone on the stage. The first time I'm lonely, the second time I'm not. That's a story."

I move out from behind her. "Or what if I come back and pretend to make up with you, and then I make you disappear? Start with one character, finish with another. That's a story too."

"What is your problem?" she asks.

"Hey, I'm just offering suggestions. I'm not the one with the problem."

"You're so full of it."

"You're—"

"Enough," Jack says. "We're done here."

"But we just started!" I say. "Practice is supposed to run all day today."

He shakes his head. "We're done." He sits on the couch and starts flipping through an old issue of *Magic* magazine with Neil Patrick Harris on the cover. After a few pages he glances up. "Are you two still here?"

Zoe goes still. "Wait—you mean, *done*? As in over?"

"I'm cutting my losses." He goes back to his magazine.

I feel like I just swallowed one of Zoe's ninja rings. "You can't—just like that? Out of nowhere?"

"I told you, no drama. I'm here to train magicians, not babysit squabbling kids. Out you go. Take a walk or something. If you sort it out, come back Tuesday." He looks straight at me. "Both of you. Or don't bother."

Feeling unsteady, I follow Zoe outside. For once it's not raining, just overcast and cold. There are no people around, only scattered cars in the parking lot of the storage garage.

"Now what?" I ask.

She glares and starts walking away. I kick the wall. Now I have a sore foot and she has a head start.

"Zoe, wait," I call.

She turns around. There are tears on her face, but she holds her head up high. "Were you trying to make me quit? Is that what this is about?"

I pause, still ten feet away from her. "What? No. No, that's not what I was trying to do." At least, today it wasn't. "Look, you can't blame me for not wanting to spend the whole routine offstage."

"God forbid you're out of the spotlight for thirty seconds."

Is that how she sees me? "I've worked hard to get good at magic," I say slowly. "Really hard. For a lot of years now. How long have you been at it?"

"A little over a year."

"Right. And you think it's fair that I spend half the routine offstage when I'm the better magician?"

"How long have you been performing, Alex? Since you were six? Because I have. Maybe you know more card tricks, but I belong on that stage as much as you do."

"Performing what?"

"It's none of your business." She closes around the words like a shell.

None of this is going the way I wanted. I wish Hakim were here. He'd know what to say. "You brought it up. What, were you an actor or something?"

"Dancer." She glares at me.

"Fine. Great. But that's not the same thing as magic. You get that, right? This is a magic competition. We're not going to win with you up there doing first-year tricks."

"Jack thinks we will."

"In case you didn't notice, Jack just kicked us out."

"So now nobody gets stage time. Happy?"

If we were closer to the wall, I'd kick it again. "Of course not." I take a deep breath. "Look, are we going to do this? Are we going to try to sort it out?"

"Because Jack says it's both or none?"

Because if we don't, we both lose. I take a few steps toward her. "Jack teamed us up for a reason. We could be really good together. Don't you want to win this thing?"

She wipes her face with the back of her hand. "Yeah, I do."

"So let's work it out. I'll buy you coffee or something."

"Forget it. I don't want to look at you across a table anytime soon." Her shoulders soften. Just a little. "Too much like our routine."

I smile. Just a little. "And you'd yank the cloth off the table all magician-style, and that always gets awkward."

There's a pause, and then she cracks the tiniest sliver of a smile back at me. "Please. I can do it without spilling a grain of salt."

"It's not the salt I'm worried about. What if you make me disappear?" But she's right. A restaurant is no good. I don't want to sit and talk. I want to be doing something. I have an idea.

"Do you want to see the stage we'll be competing on?"

Nine

As we head out of the parking lot, a silver pickup truck pulls in and parks. A man around my dad's age jumps out and heads for Jack's door. I turn to watch.

He's tall and thin, with dark skin and short hair, and wears a dressy leather coat. If he's a magician, I don't recognize him. "Who do you think that is?"

Zoe shrugs. "Jack's allowed to have friends, right?"

The man knocks three times quickly, barely pauses and then pounds again, louder. He's not acting like a friend. "Hold on," I tell Zoe.

Jack's door rolls open. He and the man shake hands warmly, and the tension in my shoulders drains away. They speak for a moment, and then Jack nods and follows the man to the truck.

They pass us as they drive out of the lot, but Jack either doesn't notice us or pretends not to.

"What do you think that was all about?"

Zoe shakes her head and starts walking. "Nosy much?"

The hotel where the competition will be held isn't far from where we are. At first we don't talk, and then Zoe asks how I know we'll be able to get in.

"It's a hotel. People walk in all the time."

"But how do you know the stage room will be open?"

I smile. "It won't be. The manager is a magician. I know her from Donna's shop." As soon as I found out where the competition was being held, I started visiting every few weeks.

A smile breaks across Zoe's face. "Cool. Let's go."

We walk in silence for a few minutes, but this isn't getting us any closer to knowing each other or working together. "What kind of dance?" I ask.

"What?"

"You said you were a dancer. There're different kinds, right?"

"Oh." She stuffs her hands in her coat pockets. "I did ballet, mostly."

"Why *did*? You don't dance anymore?"

"No." Her eyes are fixed on the sidewalk.

"How come?"

"Car accident."

The words hang between us for a few steps while I fumble for words. "I'm sorry."

She shrugs. "There's a ballet school in Winnipeg. It's a pretty big deal. That's where I went. My mom came out to visit me a year ago last Thanksgiving, and a truck ran a stop sign and plowed into my side of the car." She takes a deep breath. "It's the *prairies*. You can watch your dog run away for two days. You'd think he'd have seen us."

I can't tell if the dog thing is supposed to be a joke. None of this is funny. "So now you can't dance?"

"Torn ACL." She reaches down and raps the side of her right knee, so I know what she means. "The leg was broken too, but the ACL is why I have to wear a knee brace. No more ballet, at least not at the level I was dancing at. So I quit."

"And you started doing magic instead?"

"I had bad whiplash too. It affected the nerves in my left arm. I couldn't use it properly for a long time. Remember when I told you about magic being used as physiotherapy? It gave me something to work toward." The flat, unemotional way she tells it is worse than if she was crying.

"It sucks that that happened to you." I'm reaching for the right words. They come slowly. "I'm glad you found magic."

We walk another half block before she answers. "Thanks."

When we reach the hotel, we're in luck. Angela, the manager, is behind the desk. "Nice to see you again, Alex. Who's your friend?"

I introduce Zoe, and Angela shakes her hand. "It's always great to meet another female magician," she says, winking. "There aren't nearly enough of us."

Angela shows us to the room and unlocks the door, then leaves us alone. The room is like a small theater. It's weird to have something like this in a hotel, but when I asked Angela about it, she said they host a lot of conferences. Anyhow, it's a proper stage, curtains and all. We enter at the back and stand behind the plush seats, looking down at the stage.

"The raised seats will mess up your sight lines if you're not ready for it," I say. "And stage left, up near the front, there's a board that squeaks. See? We've got home-field advantage."

Her hand runs along the top of one of the chair backs, the one on the end of the row. "Sure, but right now we haven't got a routine. Not one we can both live with, anyhow."

When the idea hits, it feels so right that I wonder if it was where I was heading all along without knowing it. "We've got a stage. Let's work it out."

So for the next hour, that's what we do. We go through the routine piece by piece, not filling in all the tricks and details, but working through the story. And what we come up with, I think, is better than what Jack had us doing. It's not a love story. It starts out that way, but that's not how it ends.

It's about two people becoming a team.

I still have to hide behind the table.

But now I can live with it.

Ten

When I get to Donna's shop the next day, Jack is there, leaning against the counter. He doesn't bat an eye when I come in. It's like he was waiting for me.

He raises his overgrown eyebrows. I meet his gaze, hold it for a second and then nod. A smile spreads across his face. "I'll see you Tuesday, then." He says goodbye to Donna and leaves.

Donna has Cleopatra eye makeup today. "I take it things are resolved?"

"He told you?"

"He knew I'd be interested," Donna says. "I'm glad to hear you've worked it out. So, show me what you've been working on."

It's her usual Sunday question. Today I show her a flashy shuffle that Jack introduced me to.

"He's a good teacher, isn't he?" I say. I wonder what it was like having Jack for a father. Having a dad who cared about magic.

"The best." She hesitates. "I'd have asked him to judge the contest instead of Bayard if I'd had any idea he'd say yes. He doesn't usually get involved with anything that might tie him down." Something flashes across her face, but it's gone before I can read it.

"Why do you think he's working with us?" It's something I've been wondering about. We're splitting the prize money, but I'm not stupid enough to believe that Jack would put all these hours in for a couple hundred dollars.

Donna wipes the counter with a cloth. "I'm sure he has his reasons."

The copper bells over the door jingle. It's Callum, wearing a pleather jacket that I've never seen on him before. He's done something weird with his hair too. It's kind of parted in the middle and hanging down on each side.

Donna had looked up with a smile, the way she always does when someone enters the store, but as she takes in Callum with his fake-leather jacket and his weird hairdo, her smile fades.

That's when I realize who he's supposed to look like. Bayard Bellini. I find myself wishing Zoe could see, but she's home studying.

"Alex, my man! How's it going?" He's laying on the fake friendly, putting on a show for Donna.

"Hey, Callum. Congratulations, by the way." I shake his hand. Now it's a be-friendly contest. I force a smile.

"Thanks," Callum says. "It's great working with a top-level magician like Bayard. We've worked out a whole new routine, some real modern stuff. Just call me Callum Blaine." He grins.

I pretend not to get it. "That's your middle name? Blaine?"

"No." His face falls. "I was just kidding. Because, you know, David Blaine. *The* David Blaine? So I said, just call me Callum Blaine. It's a joke."

Donna swats at me, and her dozen or so bracelets clatter. "Glad to hear things are going well, Callum."

And then it's Sunday as usual. The other kids trickle in. We show each other what we've been working on. Paul has some ambitious card stuff

I haven't seen him do before. I show him a grip that Jack's been working on with me.

What I hear from the other kids, over and over, is that I've gotten better. In just a few practices, I've gotten better.

There are still two months to go before the competition.

*   *   *

At dinner, Mom asks how the practices are going. I don't want to talk about the way things almost fell apart, so instead I talk about Zoe. About what happened to her, and her learning magic through physio.

Dad leans forward. "Her physiotherapist recommended this? Fascinating."

I nod. "People get frustrated if they have to learn to tie their shoelaces again, but you can learn a coin trick and that helps you develop the same kind of finger movements. It's cool."

Dad asks lots of questions about the way magic is used in therapy. Some of them are the same questions I asked Zoe on the bus ride home from the hotel. I like the fact that I sound smart when I'm answering him.

"It's good to see you developing an interest in the practical side of this," Dad says. He avoids the word *magic*. "I didn't take you seriously when you said you wanted to be a physiotherapist. I apologize."

My knife scrapes against my plate. When did I ever say that? I want to be a magician. That's all. But Dad hasn't been so excited to talk to me in years. "I'm thinking about it," I lie.

He tells me the names of some of the muscles in the hand, and I show how I can move them. His hands are gymnasts too. Like mine. Surgeon's hands.

We sit at the table even after dinner's done, talking until Dad's phone calls him away.

I head up to my room and close the door. My backpack glowers at me from beside the desk. I pull the quiz out of the side pocket.

F. Failure. Fraud.

I forge Dad's signature.

Eleven

Tuesday's practice is better. Zoe and I work through the opening sequence, watching ourselves in the broken mirrors. "Again," Jack says, pacing.

"Do you believe in love?" Zoe asks the imaginary audience as I stand frozen in the background. "They say that when two people are meant to be together, they know." Two ninja rings slide magically into each other. "But what if that's not true?" The rings come apart. Two solid circles. She taps them against each other.

"I was happy on my own." She does some of the showier tricks from her routine, bringing out all five rings and linking them into a flower, a butterfly, a chain. "And then I met a boy."

My turn. I unfreeze, practicing some one-handed cuts, pretending not to notice Zoe.

"Too slow," Jack calls. "When she says 'boy,' you need to be stepping forward. No pause."

We try again. This time I get as far as the part when I look up and see Zoe, and the cards spring from my bottom hand to my top hand.

"Make it bigger," Jack says. He positions my hands farther apart. "And square yourself to the audience. Make eye contact with the judges. You don't need to be facing Zoe at this point. You've spotted her. Now you're including the audience in your reaction. Slow down."

It's hard. And repetitive. I have to physically learn each key position—where I am on the stage and in relation to Zoe, whether I'm standing tall or slouching, where my hands and legs are, even the expression on my face. Muscle memory, Jack calls it.

"I-am-a-ro-bot," I joke.

Jack frowns. "You learn it, and then you can play with it. You've got a long way to go."

He backs off me for a bit and goes to work with Zoe on some of her new tricks. She's way better at the muscle-memory thing than I am, probably because of all the dance training. I walk through my positions. While I do it, my brain is busy. My essay plan is due on Friday. I read *The Great Gatsby* all the way to the end, but I don't know what I'm supposed to say about it. I thought Gatsby was cool for a while, but he turned out to be kind of sad.

"Alex," Jack calls. "Cards."

I glance down and catch my hands in mid-shuffle.

*   *   *

"Can a non-magician sit at this table?" Hakim asks Zoe and me.

I slide my tray to one side to make room. "Who's a non-magician? Zoe, you should see this man's Houdini change. Only you can't, because his move is practically invisible."

The Houdini change is a move where you switch one card for another on top of the deck. I used to call it the Erdnase change, but Jack says Houdini invented it. Jack's like a walking dictionary of who invented which card trick. I never cared before.

Hakim grins at the compliment and drops into an empty chair. "He wouldn't be laying it on so thick if we didn't have an English assignment due," he tells Zoe.

She laughs.

"Speaking of," I say. "Tonight?"

Hakim shakes his head. "Can't. I'm seeing a movie with some of the softball guys. How about Thursday?"

"I have practice."

Hakim looks worried. "I guess I can wait to see the movie."

I glance at Zoe. She doesn't need to know what a dunce I am. "Relax. My essay plan is not your problem. Anyhow, I got it under control."

Hakim whistles low. "I think a pig somewhere just sprouted wings."

* * *

Friday, I walk into English class and see a stack of essay plans on Mrs. Forsythe's desk. I stop still.

I'm a dead man.

She's not here yet. It's better to hand in garbage than not hand in anything at all. At least this way I can pretend that I misunderstood her instructions. It's not as if it's the real essay; this is just the plan. I rush to my desk, tear a blank piece of paper out of my binder and scrawl on it *Essay Topic—Who Was Gatsby Really?* I add, *Can we ever really know a person?* and sign my name, then stick it under the top paper in the pile, out of sight.

"Seriously?" Hakim asks me.

"Shut up."

He shakes his head. "It was nice knowing you."

Twelve

Saturday morning, I'm still waiting for the ax to fall.

I go to practice at Jack's studio but screw up every second move. When Jack tries to correct my shuffle, I drop the cards all over the floor—52 Pickup.

"What's with you today?" Jack asks.

"I'm not feeling great," I lie. I wipe my arm across my forehead. "I might be coming down with something."

He frowns. "Don't. We haven't got time for that."

We work on the final visual moment of the routine, where Zoe and I link a bunch of rings together into a long chain and give them a half twist so we can arch them up into a rainbow shape over the table. Beneath them, what looks like a jumble of cards rises up into a prefab card castle.

"Don't you think it looks kind of...fairy-tale?" I ask.

Jack didn't fuss when Zoe and I made changes to the tone of the routine, but to me, the castle thing feels like a throwback to the romance line.

"It's all right," Zoe says. "Think of it as magical, not fairy-tale. You know—the Magic Castle, in California."

"It's too cold in here to be California," I grumble.

Jack shakes his head. "It's symbolic—the rings and the cards coming together. The judges will love it. You want to be a competition magician, this is the game you have to play. That is, if you're sure this is what you want."

"What do you mean?" Of course it's what I want. It's what I've always wanted. Alex Eisen, world champion.

The thought doesn't warm me like it usually does. I push it aside and focus on Jack.

Jack studies me for a moment. "There are other ways of being a magician besides competition." He draws himself up, all business again. "Remember, you two, you're looking at the judges here. Make eye contact with someone, then move your eyes up to the arch of rings. That's how you draw them in and show them where to look."

We break for lunch. Zoe and I walk to a nearby sub shop. "Something's bugging you," she says. "Is it the routine?"

I shake my head. "School stuff. That's all."

"You know, we did *Gatsby* at my school last year. My old school," she corrects herself. "If there's anything I can do to help—"

Write my essay for me. "Thanks. I'll be okay. Just have to muscle through it."

That's Dad's expression, *muscle through it.* I can't believe the words just left my mouth.

After lunch, Jack has us walk through the full routine, start to finish. I'm on. I can feel it. I'm making my gestures big, pausing at the good visual moments to let the audience see what's happening. Jack has cut nearly all of our patter, letting the magic speak for itself. At the end, when Zoe and I create the card castle, there's a moment. I can feel it. We've cast a spell.

Jack nods slowly. "Better," he says. "Not quite there yet, but better. Now we can get started."

"Get started?" I ask.

"I'm going to book some shows for us, starting week after next. We need to run through it with an audience. See what parts get the laughs, see what falls flat. Then we can tweak it."

"We're taking the routine live?" Zoe lights up.

Excitement fizzes inside me. I've done a few birthday parties, but other than at Donna's shop, I haven't really performed that much. Not for strangers. Never as part of a team, and never with my magic as good as it is now.

"Enjoy this part, kids." Jack winks. "This is the part where you learn real magic."

I have the entire bus ride home to feel good about the changes to the routine. That and the first ten seconds after I walk through the back door. That's how long it takes for Mom to find me.

"Your English teacher called," she says.

Thirteen

I'm out. Out of the competition. Out of magic.

Sunday morning, I sit on the corner of my bed, flicking cards from one hand to the other. This deck is about a month old, just broken in nicely. Not too sticky, not too slick.

This is the first Sunday since Christmas holidays that I'm not going to Donna's. At least I won't have to see what Callum Blaine is working on this week for his competition routine.

Mom knocks on my door. "Phone for you." She holds out the cordless. Weird. All my friends have my cell number.

It's Jack. "I heard what happened," he says. I called Zoe last night; she must have tracked him down.

"I'm really sorry," I say.

"I bet. I'd be too, in your shoes."

I pause. "So are you going to go ahead with just Zoe?"

"I'm going to go ahead with both of you, just like we planned, as soon as you get your act together."

"I can't do magic anymore." I hate that he's making me say it.

"Didn't think you'd fold so fast."

"You don't know my dad. He won't let me compete."

There's silence on the other end of the line. "That's as may be," he says finally. "But here's something to keep in mind. This competition isn't the be-all and end-all of magic. Funny thing is, I'm not even a fan of magic competitions in the first place. That's not what magic's all about."

"What do you mean?"

"When you compete, you're forcing it—doing things just to get points from the judges. Performing magic for a real audience, that's something else entirely. That's a gift, from you to them."

"Then why are you sponsoring us, if you don't like competitions?"

He sighs. "What I'm trying to say is, magic's in your blood. You'll find a way to perform. But for now, I think you know what you have to do."

"Get my act together."

"You gotta earn the magic."

After he hangs up, I toss the phone from one hand to the other a few times, then drop it onto my bed. I dig *Gatsby* out of my backpack and unearth a ruler from the piles of papers and cards on my desk. And then I sit down to work.

* * *

Monday after school, Mom, Dad and Mrs. Forsythe gather in the English classroom, at my request. Dad keeps looking at his watch. I'm not sure what Mom had to promise to make him be here.

Deep breath. This might be the most important performance of my life. Zoe helped me come up with the idea—I'm not going to tell my parents what magic means to me. I'm going to show them.

Facing my audience, I raise both hands, palms outward. No secrets. "I screwed up. No arguments from me. And I'm going to get caught up."

Mrs. Forsythe nods.

I continue. "But in the meantime, I want to show you why I should be allowed to keep doing magic." I reach into my backpack.

Dad groans. "If this is a card trick..."

"It isn't."

Mom leans forward.

I pull out my grade-three report card. "*Painfully shy*," I read. "*Has difficulty participating. Reading well below grade level. Needs encouragement to reach his potential.*"

Mom looks stricken. She reaches for the report card, so I hand it to her. She folds it and places it back in its brown envelope, then holds it against her chest.

I cover grade four the same way. The comments are mostly the same. *Alex keeps to himself. Easily distracted.*

"Grade five, end of year. *Alex has come out of his shell.*" I look at them each in turn, drawing their attention back to the paper in my hands. Using eye contact to connect them to what I want them to pay attention to, like Jack taught me. "It says *Reading below grade level*," I admit. "But it also says *Alex is making an effort to partic-ipate in class discussions. His overall performance is much improved.* And look—the grades are higher. Some of them."

I hold the report card out to Dad. He makes no move to take it.

"It got better in grade six. But grade five was the year—do you remember what I got for my birthday that year?" I set the report card on the desk in front of me, as if that were my plan all along. It lands with a slight tremble. "Do you?"

"Magic kit," Mom whispers.

Mrs. Forsythe claps. "Alex, I applaud your presentation skills. You've made a strong argument. There's nothing I enjoy more than seeing students pursuing their dreams, as long as the schoolwork doesn't suffer. This decision, however, rests with your parents. I'll leave you in private to discuss it."

Once the door closes, Dad speaks. "Your coach has been in touch with your mother," he says. "He extended his apologies and communicated his respect for our decision. And he requested that you be permitted to honor certain show bookings that he has made, as a form of volunteer work in the community. You would rehearse Saturday mornings and present Saturday afternoons."

I feel myself grow still. "What did you say?"

"We agreed," Mom says. "As long as your grades stay up. You'll check in with Mrs. Forsythe once a week, to make sure you're on top of your schoolwork."

"And the competition?"

Mom shakes her head. "One thing at a time."

"Are we done here?" Dad steps away from the table. As he reaches the door, he turns back to face us but doesn't meet my eyes. "As it happens, I already knew about one of the bookings. It's for the children's ward at my hospital. I thought I might watch."

Fourteen

"**I** hate hospitals," Zoe mutters. For the tenth time.

The common room in the children's wing at the hospital is about the size of a large classroom, and murals are painted on all the walls. I know, because I've been looking around the room for twenty minutes now, waiting for Jack to show up.

One wall is a rain forest, one's an underwater ocean scene. The wall with the windows has kites and birds flitting between them, and the blue sky and puffy clouds spill over onto the ceiling. The last wall is fireworks, which turn into stars and then rockets zooming into outer space.

It all makes me dizzy.

"I can't believe he's not here," I whisper to Zoe. "It's our first show."

"Maybe he wants us to know we can do it on our own."

"He was supposed to bring the table."

She shrugs, but since the nurses are starting to bring in the kids, she pastes a smile on her face and greets them instead of answering me.

Some of the kids sit on the floor; some sit on plastic kindergarten-sized chairs. Some of the kids are in wheelchairs, and some come with their own IV poles.

"You okay?" Zoe whispers.

I nod. But the skinny, bald, six-year-old girl is breaking my heart. Her teddy bear is bald too. It looks like someone shaved it. A boy who can't be much younger than Zoe and me sneers, like he's daring me to feel sorry for him. He's leaning back on his chair, looking as bored and cool as it's possible to look when you're wearing a blue hospital gown.

We have ten kids all together. Which is good, because it means I have more than enough balloons. I bought some just for this and learned a couple of balloon-animal twists off the Internet. I can do dog, giraffe and bunny.

I pull out a balloon and start stretching it.

"No latex," Cool Boy says.

"What?"

"No latex balloons allowed." He's caught a nurse's attention now, and she confirms what he said.

"Oh. Okay." I put the balloon bag away. Teddy Bear Girl looks disappointed.

"I hate hospitals," Zoe mutters. *Eleven.*

It's not a great start to our routine, but we have their attention now. Dad's not here yet. It figures. "So hi," I start. "I'm Alex, and this is Zoe. How are we all doing today?"

There's silence in the room. "It's a hospital," Cool Boy says. "How do you think we're doing?"

"Lucas," one of the nurses warns.

Zoe takes a deep breath and steps forward. "I spent some time in a hospital not that long ago. You know what the worst part was?" She pauses and makes eye contact, like Jack taught us.

"No dogs!" Teddy Bear Girl says.

"The food," another boy calls.

"Needles," another says.

"Chemo," Lucas says. Which puts a damper on the room.

"I got bored," Zoe says, undeterred. "You're stuck in a room, and you feel horrible, and sometimes you can sleep and sometimes not, but the days are all the same."

A couple of the kids nod.

She holds up six cards for the kids to see. "How many cards?" They count together. At least, the little ones do.

"Right. Let's pretend each one is an hour of hospital time. So say you have a visitor for one hour." She moves one card to the front of the deck. "And then you sleep for two." She discards two. "How many hours are left?"

She should have four cards in her hand. She still has six. She runs through the process three more times, and even though she discards more and more cards, she always has six cards left. "Doesn't it feel like that sometimes? Like the days go on forever?"

More nods.

"So Alex and I are going to see if we can make this hour a little more interesting for you. Does that sound good?"

"Yes!" a couple of the younger kids yell.

We don't start out with our joint routine; we save that for the end. I do my Weird Science bit first, and a few audience-participation card tricks, and then Zoe does some card tricks of her own. She finishes up with her hoops. Teddy Bear Girl watches her like she's a rock star.

Then we get to the routine. It's a little modified, because I can't disappear behind the folding card table we borrowed, so Zoe turns me into a statue instead. It's the best ad-lib we could come up with on short notice. I'm actually disappointed not to be able to disappear, because Teddy Bear Girl probably would have thought it was cool. It bothers me that they're not getting our whole routine, so I put everything I have into the bits we *can* do.

By the end, when we raise our card castle under the magic rings, even Lucas is leaning forward. As the other kids are leaving, he asks me to show him a card trick. I walk him through a basic double lift and give him one of my spare decks to practice with.

"I could come back sometime, if you want," I offer. "To see how you're doing and maybe teach you something else." I don't know why I say it. I don't even know this kid. But I'm remembering what Zoe said, about being in the hospital and about using magic for physiotherapy. Maybe physio isn't the only thing magic is good for.

"Cool," he says.

Something makes me lift my eyes to the back of the room. Dad's there. He missed the routine, but he's been watching me with Lucas. He stands there for another moment. And then he disappears.

Fifteen

We do a few shows at local restaurants and one at a retirement home. One for a group of Girl Guides, one at a local branch of the Canadian Legion and one at a fund-raising event for a pet shelter. Jack comes to all of them. After each show he goes over the routine with us, and we discuss what worked and what didn't. We make changes.

He never does explain what happened with the hospital show, only that he had somewhere else he needed to be.

It's hard doing the routine in different spaces, watching our angles, reading the audience, but we get pretty good at adapting. We leave out whatever we need to leave out. And if one of us is struggling or forgets a line or fumbles a trick, the other usually finds some way to fill in.

"How do you like it?" Jack asks me after the retirement-home show, near the end of April.

"Like what?"

His eyes glint. "Performing."

It turns out I like it a lot.

*   *   *

After school one day, Zoe corners me. "We need to know, Alex. Are you going to be allowed to compete?"

I hang my head. "I got my essay back from Mrs. Forsythe today."

"And?"

"B minus."

She hesitates. "And that's—?"

"Are you kidding?" I grab her by the shoulders and spin her around. "I'm a genius!"

She's laughing. People are staring. I don't care.

"Alex, my knee. Take it easy." She squeezes my arms, pulls back and then launches a giant hug at me. "I'm so proud of you!"

Mom and Dad have to let me compete after this. I pull the essay out of my backpack—*Can You Ever Really Know Someone?* by Alex Eisen—and kiss it. "I'm back, baby."

"You'd better have been talking to the essay," Zoe says.

"I was."

* * *

Two weeks before the competition, Zoe and I are at Donna's for the magic group on Sunday afternoon. Donna's asked us, and Callum too, to perform our competition routines for the other kids. And to let them see the debriefing part, where we talk it over and give each other feedback. The kids are going to offer us feedback as well. Plastic chairs form a circle around the stage.

"Is it awesome, working with Jack?" Paul asks. He's sitting on my left, Zoe on my right. "It must be awesome."

I'm thinking about the lady at the retirement home who couldn't stop clapping, her face as bright and open as a summer sky. And about Lucas, whose ambitious card routine is coming along well. "It's awesome."

Donna keeps looking at the door, but Jack still hasn't arrived. So we don't have our table—again. Donna lets us borrow a similar one that she has on display in the store.

Callum and Bayard stroll in five minutes before the show starts. Bayard's wearing jeans, a leather jacket and a button-up shirt that's mostly not buttoned. Callum's his Mini-Me.

Paul snorts. "Bellini and Baloney."

As they move into the store, Bayard steps away from Callum, as if he's trying to distance himself.

Callum sidles up beside Zoe. "Want to see something?" Before she can answer, he launches into a four-card switch that blows my mind. "And that's nothing. That's not even in the routine."

I swallow. But Zoe just stands up, so they're at eye level. "That was nice, Callum. I can't wait to see your other stuff." Her voice is cool.

"Nice?" He flushes. "Nice?"

"Pretty. I think there are still some seats open over there, if you want to go check your stuff."

She sits back down next to me as he leaves. "He's just trying to game you, Alex. I've seen it before. Dancer, remember? Girls would always come up and try to intimidate you before a competition."

Vicious ballerinas? "They do that?"

"Not the ones who matter."

What will you do to win? As soon as it flashes through my head, I realize it's been a long time since I thought that way. And I know the answer now, or part of it—I know what I wouldn't do. I wouldn't do what Callum's doing.

Callum, when he performs, is perfect. He does a lot of Bayard's stuff and some card work that I've seen him do before. He's practiced and polished and smooth. The patter never lets up, and neither do the tricks. It's a whirlwind of magic. He uses the whole stage. He's fast. He's funny. Or at least you can tell he's supposed to be funny, and you know when to laugh.

But there's something...robotic about the routine. It's like he's just going through the motions. A lot of his gestures are ones that Bayard uses. And I shift in my too-hard plastic chair, because there's something uncomfortably familiar about the way Callum keeps piling on more and more tricks. There's no real connection. It's like we're supposed to look at the magic, not at him.

It's the way I used to perform.

And the other kids pick up on it. Callum gets comments like "Cool trick" and "Great effect," but a couple of kids also say they got confused and had trouble following his routine.

Callum looks at me. "What did you think?" His tone dares me to criticize.

I feel Donna's eyes on me. "It's good," I say.

"But?"

"Well...it feels like maybe you're forcing it."

"What's that supposed to mean? Forcing what?"

"Like you're performing for points, not people."

"So?"

When Zoe and I go up, I make sure to walk slowly. I remind myself to display each effect, and to make eye contact with every single person. Even Callum.

Once, I drop the cards by accident. "That got my attention," says Zoe. And the line, which usually goes with a flourish I'm supposed to do, works even better when it's used for a fumble. We get a laugh.

And once, Zoe throws wide and a ninja ring lands offstage. "Feel free to examine that," I say as Paul hands it back. "No gimmicks, right?"

We're not forcing it, not even a little. We're performing, as best we can, for the people watching. And they love it. At the end, when we raise the card castle, there's a moment of silence before the applause.

The critique picks up on little things. Our mistakes get mentioned. But mostly they loved it.

"Good showmanship."

"I really liked the way you displayed that effect up high, so everyone could see it."

"Nice pacing."

"Funny."

Donna compliments Zoe on her poise. "You looked very professional up there. Stick with it, sister."

Zoe smiles.

Bayard approaches me afterward. "You okay with this whole double-act thing?"

Still high from performing, I grin. "Yeah. Zoe's great. We make a good team."

"Last time I saw you perform, you got more stage time, if you know what I mean."

"Maybe," I say. "But I didn't know what to do with it."

Bayard studies me. "If you decide you want to jump ship, you let me know."

"A man backs the wrong horse, he still has to see the race through." It's Jack.

From the look on Bayard's face, he's as surprised as I am to see Jack standing behind us. "Well, you'd know, wouldn't you?"

Jack says nothing. Bayard walks away.

"Where were you?" I ask.

"I had a meeting."

Donna comes and steals him away, and I find Zoe. I don't want to work with Bayard. It feels wrong, and besides, I don't think he's done Callum any favors.

But Bayard's words bring back the picture, the way I used to imagine my life as a magician. Me, on a stage, astonishing people. My name in lights.

Only mine.

Sixteen

It's the last Saturday before the competition. Zoe and I take the bus to Jack's studio together. He's not there, but we know the code to open the door: 2157, the same as the street address of Donna's store.

Inside, things have changed. The shabby furniture is still there, but all of the illusion pieces he was building are gone and the tools are nowhere in sight. It's dark and cold inside. No surprise; Vancouver's on its sixth or seventh straight day of drizzle. I've lost track.

We run through the routine a couple of times and then settle in on the couch to wait.

"How's the school stuff coming?" Zoe asks, leaning against the armrest.

I roll my eyes. "Good. Thanks, Mom."

She flicks a card at me. "I'm just sayin'. I don't want to lose my favorite partner the week before the competition."

I flick it back. "You have a not-favorite partner?"

"My backup, Ernest. I keep him in the trunk, just in case you screw up." She nudges Jack's World War II coffee table with her toe.

"I screw up all the time."

"True. Better get him out, then." She leans over and opens the trunk. "Come on, Ernest."

There are lots of papers and old magazines in the trunk. I don't know why my eye falls on the yellow pamphlet. *BNDY 90 DSYA*, it says. Or something like that. There's a large *GA* at the bottom.

Zoe lets the trunk fall shut. From the look on her face, I know she's seen something bad. My stomach flips.

"What is it?" I ask. "Show me." I open the trunk.

"I didn't mean—" she starts. But she picks up the pamphlet.

"I know. Tell me what it says."

"*Beyond 90 Days.* And the small print at the bottom says *Gamblers Anonymous.*" She places the pamphlet back onto the stack of papers and closes the lid of the trunk.

Once you see something, you can't un-see it.

"It might not be his," Zoe tries.

"Sure." Jack as a gambler? It's not hard to picture. For half a second, I wonder if that's why he left magic. Magicians perform in casinos all the time.

It doesn't matter, I decide. It's Jack's business, not ours. The main thing is, he can't ever know we were snooping through his stuff. Even accidentally.

We do card tricks for each other, waiting for Jack. We've seen the tricks before, but we pretend we haven't.

Lunchtime rolls around. Still no Jack. Neither one of us has a phone number for him. We go for subs, come back and eat them, then run through the routine a couple more times.

"We should tell someone," Zoe says. "What if he's been in an accident or something?"

I dial the store. One of Donna's employees answers. "I'm sorry, Donna's not in today."

On a Saturday? Maybe something really has happened to Jack. "Can you give me her home number?"

"Alex, you know I can't do that."

But Zoe's already on her cell. "I found her," she says, showing me a listing on her browser. She calls it but hands me the phone before Donna picks up.

"Hello?" Donna sounds like she has a cold.

"Donna? It's Alex Eisen. I...listen, this is kind of weird, but do you have a number for Jack? He's not here, and he's supposed to be. He's never missed a practice before. There was that time at the hospital, but it was a show."

I know that I'm babbling and making zero sense. So it's weird when Donna says, "I know."

"You...know? Know what, where Jack is?"

"Not that. Nobody knows that." Silence sits heavy on the line. "Alex, Jack is—well, he's missing."

Seventeen

onna invites us to her apartment. It's not far from the store. We take the SkyTrain down. Donna lives on the third floor of a yellow stucco walk-up near the water. She opens the door wearing jeans and a plain gray sweatshirt, with her hair in a ponytail. Bare feet. No high heels or glittery bracelets. I blink. For the first time, it occurs to me that Donna-at-the-store might not be the same as Donna-at-home. That she might be playing a character, just like magicians do onstage.

There's a man with her. It takes me a moment to recognize him as the man we saw in the parking lot at Jack's place the day that Zoe and I went to the hotel. "This is Michael, Jack's sponsor," she says. "From Jack's support group for people with gambling addictions."

Zoe and I look at each other. I know she's thinking about the pamphlet we found.

Donna invites us in and pours lemonade from a glass pitcher. She and Michael ask us when we last saw Jack. Where it was and for how long. They ask about our practices and our shows, which ones he was at and which ones he missed. Michael writes it down. "In case there's anything here the police can use," Donna says.

"The police are looking for him?" Somehow that makes it more real. There's a hollow feeling in my chest.

Donna nods. "He's been gone since—" Her voice breaks, and she takes a drink of lemonade. When she starts again, her voice is under control. "He was last seen at a casino."

So it's not just that he missed a practice. It's not just that he's missing today. He's disappeared, in a way I can't wrap my mind around. I suddenly realize that I've got my cards in my hands again, shuffling. Jack's not here to call me on it.

I want to ask what this means for Zoe and me, for the magic competition, but even in my own head that sounds selfish, so I say nothing.

Michael walks us to the stairwell.

I feel like I can ask him the things I didn't want to ask Donna. "What do they think happened?"

He leans against the wall. "They really don't know."

"What do *you* think happened?" Zoe asks.

Michael's eyes go distant. "Gamblers cover for one another. So it's possible that he's staying with someone and will reappear when he's ready. I've been asking around." He sighs. "Against my advice, Jack had stopped coming to meetings."

I have to know. "When were the meetings?"

Michael blinks. "Well, nearly every day, in some part of town. But the one Jack and I attended regularly was on Saturday mornings." His eyes snap to my face. He makes the connection at the same time I do. "This is not your fault. Jack was dealing with a difficult problem in the best way he knew how. He made his own choices. You are not responsible for them."

Zoe and I go online as soon as we're out of the building. We find out that there's an official missing-persons bulletin out for Jack and that his wallet was found in the casino's parking lot.

We find out that gambling has the highest suicide rate of all the addictions.

"He'll be back," Zoe says. "He won't miss the competition."

"Sure." I shuffle my cards, flipping them up at random until I find the one I'm looking for.

It's his card.

Eighteen

Donna drives Zoe and me to the competition. We have to go early, to sign in. Mom and Dad are coming later with Hakim.

Our equipment barely fits in the trunk of Donna's vw hatchback; half the backseat is down to make room for the table we borrowed from the shop. I'm glad that Zoe's smaller than me and it made more sense for her to be the one crammed into the backseat.

While we're stopped at a red light, Donna glances at me. Her gold hoop earrings brush her shoulders; she could sit parrots in them. "You two are good kids. Working with you made Jack happy, you know that? I think at first he did it just to impress me, but he likes you."

"Not enough to stick around for the competition," I mutter.

The light switches to green, and Donna faces forward again. Her fingers turn white on the steering wheel. I wish I hadn't opened my mouth.

"You're angry," she says. "Me too. This isn't new, you know. He's struggled with this addiction my whole life."

"Sorry," I say. But she's right: I am angry. "Why now? It isn't that we can't do the routine without him. We can. It just would have been nice to finish as a team. We've been working together for months, and he couldn't stick around for one more week?"

"Alex—" Zoe starts.

"I want you to know something," Donna interrupts. "He was trying. Really trying. He—"

I stare out the window.

Donna sighs. "You know what? Let's talk about something different. Talk me through your routine."

But we're quiet as we walk into the hotel. There are jugglers in the lobby, and balloons at the registration table. I even see Shane Ferguson, world-champion magician, signing cards for people. I should be thrilled to be here.

We line up to register. Bayard comes over to say hello. He shakes Donna's hand. "No word from Jack?"

"Nothing yet," Donna says. "Thanks for asking."

"Of course, of course. That's too bad," Bayard says. "You know, I did take the liberty of asking about sponsor substitutions. You would have to re-register as a new team, and the deadline for that has passed."

Donna's face hardens.

"What's wrong with you?" Zoe asks. "It's her father."

"I'm only trying to help."

I step on his foot as the line moves forward. "Oops. Sorry."

When we reach the counter, it turns out Bayard is right. Donna Mancuso can't sign in Jack Spader's team. We're screwed.

"That's ridiculous," Donna says. "You're not going to deprive these two of their chance to compete because of circumstances beyond their control. I want to talk to Ben."

Ben Lee is the president of the Silver Stage Vancouver chapter. I've heard him speak at meetings. He's also Callum's father. I groan.

"What?" Zoe asks.

"I don't like our chances."

Mr. Lee and Donna greet each other like old friends. He shakes our hands. "Callum has told me all about your routine," he says. "It sounds marvelous."

I pinch my arm.

"Callum's is really good too," Zoe says. "He's doing some really tough effects."

Mr. Lee turns to me. "What do you think of Callum's act?" His eyes measure me, and I get the feeling this is some kind of test.

"He's a strong magician," I say. Mr. Lee waits. "But I wonder if he's trying too hard to be someone else."

Mr. Lee smiles sadly. "He is, Alex. That's very perceptive. He's trying very hard to be you."

I find myself wanting to check that the floor beneath my feet is solid.

Mr. Lee turns back to Donna. "Go ahead and sign them in. I'll make sure you don't run into any more objections."

Everything feels slightly surreal as we head into the conference.

*　*　*

According to the schedule, we don't perform until three o'clock. It's not even lunchtime yet. There are fourteen acts in our seventeen-and-under category, mostly individuals. I phone Mom to let her know what time to come, and then Zoe and I go exploring.

We stop at the booth for a magic camp in Ontario that I've heard about. It looks fun. At another booth, Zoe and I buy matching card clips, and I pay extra to get mine engraved with my favorite card—the ace of clubs.

I point out the famous magicians to her. Jason Fung is there, and Loren Andrews and Ron Fletcher.

"And that's nothing," I hear. "That's not even in the routine." It's Callum's voice.

I turn around and see him towering over a skinny, dark-haired boy. Callum walks away. The boy looks ready to wet himself.

"I'll be right back," I promise Zoe.

The boy's name tag says *Jean-Marc Gauthier.* I recognize it from the list—he's competing in our category. I introduce myself. "You already met Callum, huh?"

Jean-Marc nods. "He's very good."

"He's pretty good, yeah. But I bet you are too, or you wouldn't be here. Don't let him freak you out. This is part of competition." Jack's words pop into my mouth. "You gotta earn the magic."

Jean-Marc straightens.

"Show me something?" I ask.

He grins and breaks into one of the slickest coin-handling routines I've ever seen.

"Nice! Are you doing that for the judges?"

His grin widens as he shakes his head. "What I'm doing for them is better."

I show him a coin grip that Jack taught me, and he adjusts my thumb before he leaves to get ready to perform.

Nineteen

By two o'clock, I'm sweating. Most of the seventeen-and-unders we've met have been friendly. Two or three of them tried to game us the way Callum did. I let Zoe handle those ones. She seems to enjoy it.

But our routine is in an hour, and it's time to focus. We meet Donna by the door to the contestants' area. Mom, Dad and Hakim are with her, and Zoe's family too. There are introductions all around, but I'm too rattled to track them.

Somehow, even after all this time, I was sure Jack would be here. I find myself looking for him every time I turn a corner. Every time I hear a voice that might be his.

And then it's time to go backstage into the prep room. So we hug our families goodbye and Donna takes us in.

We run through the routine a few times. Finally, Donna makes us stop. "Get a drink," she says. "Use the washroom. Then come back here."

Zoe's already there when I get back.

"That's one advantage to being a female magician," Donna tells me. "No bathroom lineups at the conferences."

"I knew I should have used the ladies'," I say.

We take a seat in the hallway and wait to be called. I riffle my cards. My hands are steady. "Are you nervous?" I ask Zoe.

"Well, yeah," she says. "But I'm okay. It's good nervous."

I don't feel it. Not at all. Which is weird. By now I should be a basket case. I always start out nervous, and then I step onstage and things get better. That's just the way it works. I used to picture myself joking about it in interviews once I was famous.

I try to picture it now—Alex Eisen, world champion—but the picture's too bright, like a cartoon. Even adding Zoe's name beside mine doesn't work.

I find myself thinking instead about Lucas and the other kids in the hospital ward.

"You know the thing about judges?" Donna asks me.

"What?"

"They're people. Just go out there and give them a good show."

"Yeah. I know."

She peers at me. "Alex. Are you okay?"

"I really am." That's what scares me.

We're called backstage. Even Donna can't come with us.

When the bell rings, we have thirty seconds to get our props into position and be ready to begin our routine. Just like we practiced, Zoe carries the smaller stuff and I carry the table with the prefab card castle on it.

It's dimly lit backstage, but when I lift the table, it feels wrong. Or, rather, it feels right. This isn't the table we borrowed from Donna. It's the one Jack made for us.

Zoe's already onstage. I can't call her back. I run my hand over the tabletop as a grin grows inside me. I pull my deck out of my back pocket. The card I need is on the bottom. *Bottom dweller, he is.* I make a quick change to our props, barely finishing in time to set the table in place.

We move into position and Zoe starts the routine as soon as the lights come up. "I was happy—" She falters. She must have spotted the table. "I was happy on my own," she says, like nothing happened.

My hands start into a shuffle. I raise my head and face the audience. It's a large room, but the judges are all seated near the front. There are three of them, two men and a woman. My parents and Hakim are a few rows back, sitting with Donna. Hakim waves.

"And then I met a boy," Zoe continues.

I move through my opening steps, taking it slow, pausing on the best effects. Making eye contact with the judges. My nerves build into a ball somewhere under my diaphragm. It's the wrong time. My voice comes out wire-tight.

In the very back row, I see him. A rumpled old man in a brown coat, all by himself.

Zoe smiles at me, and I can tell she already knows.

He leans forward, resting his arms on the seat in front of him. I can't make eye contact with him;

he's too far away. But I can let him know. Let him see that he made a difference.

I take a breath, and I'm not on the competition stage. I'm in the hospital room with mural-covered walls and no curtains to hide behind. And I'm connecting. I'm making the impossible happen. Not to fool anyone, and not to impress any judges. To make people smile.

I'm making magic.

I open my eyes and Zoe and I move into our card routine.

And now I feel it—stage nerves, burning bright and hot inside me, but under control. Alive with energy.

I find Dad in the audience, and I nod at him. Startled, he nods back.

I'm not here to compete.

I'm here to put on a show.

And the best is the end, the very end. I fixed the card castle. Jack is too far away to see it properly, but the man knows cards and he knows us, and when he sees a face card showing at the top of the card castle, he'll know it's not the king of clubs.

It's the jack of spades.

Twenty

H e's gone by the time we take our bows. Instantly, impossibly gone, between one glance and the next.

Backstage, Zoe and I hug one another.

Dad clears his throat. He's wearing Donna's backstage pass but holding it away from himself awkwardly, as if he's worried that someone might mistake him for Donna Mancuso and ask him about magic. "Donna gave me this and asked me to congratulate you for her. She and Jack had things to talk about. She said you'd understand."

Zoe hugs me again quickly. "I'm going to find my parents." She leaves us alone.

"You did well," Dad says as I stow our props in a quieter part of the hall. "I was a little worried for you at first, but..."

"I was a little worried for me at first too."

"You got better."

I nod.

"You know, I get nervous too. Every time I operate on someone. It's that moment right before the first incision. After that, there's a clarity, but that first cut—every single time, it gets me." He holds out his hand. Steady.

I hold out mine. It's nearly the same size. And just as steady.

"I don't know if I need to compete anymore," I tell him. I haven't made up my mind. The whole thing feels different than it used to. I wouldn't mind doing some more shows in front of people. Real people, not just judges.

"You don't have to decide today," he says. And he's right. It can wait.

"Want to learn a magic trick?" I ask.

He laughs. "Magic? Sure. Why not? You've got that young boy at the hospital baffling all the nurses with card tricks. I might as well keep up."

Maybe you can know someone after all. But that doesn't mean they can't surprise you.

"Okay," I tell him. "This is how you do a two-card lift."

*   *   *

We didn't win. But we beat Callum. And even if we hadn't, I think I'd have been okay with it.

Jean-Marc won, and I was happy for him. Really, genuinely happy. We've swapped email addresses. I hope he keeps in touch. That kid's going places.

And so am I.

Acknowledgments

First of all, thank you to my editors, Robin Stevenson and Sarah Harvey, and to my agent, Monica Pacheco. Thank you, always, to my writing friends, especially (for this novel) Susan Blakeney, Pat Bourke, Karen Krossing, Patricia McGowan, Karen Rankin, Nora Landry, Kim Moynahan, Jason Pyper, Gwynn Scheltema, Jocelyne Stone, Bill Swan and Ruth Walker.

And now the magicians. Thank you to Tom Ogden, to teen magician Dana Miettinen, to Jeff Pinsky at Browser's Den of Magic in Toronto, and most especially to Jen and "Magic" Mike Segal of Sorcerers Safari Magic Camp. Thank you to Lee Asher, Shawn Farquhar, Aaron Fisher, Justin Flom, Bobby Motta and Dan Wiebe, for letting a Muggle sit in on your teaching sessions and discussions. Thanks also to everyone else I spoke with at camp, including Ali Shelley, Alex Seaman, Chris Mayhew and Rosemary Reid. Please forgive me if I missed any names in the whirlwind of my visit! Many thanks to campers Quinton, Phil, C.J. and Griffin, "my magician friends who taught me my first double lift," and to Charles, Ben, Tyler, Mike and Jonah for talking about magic and showing me tricks. Special thanks to Phil H. for the title suggestion.

Thank you to the Poynter family, Ken, Barb, Aria and Dallas (my first teen reader!), and to Shirley Magee-Bell, physiotherapist extraordinaire. Special thanks to my cousin, Mark Dawson, for helping me with an important part of the story and feeling that it needed to be shared. And thank you, always, to my patient, supportive and inspiring family, especially Aaron and Sarah. I'm lucky to have you, and I love you all.

ERIN THOMAS is the author of six books for young readers, two of which—*Haze* and *Boarder Patrol*—are part of the Orca Sports series. She has yet to perform a successful magic trick, although she's working on a fancy card shuffle. She lives in Whitby, Ontario, with her family. For more information, visit www.erinthomas.ca.

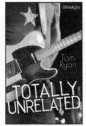